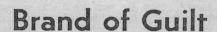

Brand of Guilt

For five long and guilty years Owen Scobey had successfully hidden his past from young Matt. And during that troubled time he had grown to love the boy as he would have loved his son. But with that love there was fear—fear of the moment when Matt would find him out, when the boy's respect and love would turn to hate.

Now that moment was close at hand. A man from Scobey's past had suddenly appeared, threatening to expose him if he would not head a cattle drive through Indian-infested country.

There was nothing Scobey could do but agree . . . agree and wait for the chance to kill the man who would destroy him.

LAW OF THE GUN

by
Lewis B. Patten

A SIGNET BOOK

NEW AMERICAN LIBRARY

SIGNET TRADEMARK REG. U.S. PAT. OFF. AND FOREIGN COUNTRIES
REGISTERED TRADEMARK—MARCA REGISTRADA
HECHO EN CHICAGO, U.S.A.

SIGNET, SIGNET CLASSIC, MENTOR, ONYX, PLUME, MERIDIAN
and NAL BOOKS are published by NAL PENGUIN INC.,
1633 Broadway, New York, New York 10019

FIRST PRINTING, MARCH, 1961

6 7 8 9 10 11 12 13 14

PRINTED IN THE UNITED STATES OF AMERICA

LAW
OF
THE
GUN

☆ 1 ☆

EMPTY it lay, a million square miles of it, sometimes flat as a table top, sometimes broken by rising escarpments of grayish sandstone, by towering pinnacles of jagged rock, or by timbered canyons in the bottom of which wound sluggish, shallow streams.

And above it the empty sky—the nearly empty sky, for there in the far distance carrion birds circled and settled and became a part of the land.

The girl would have been called plain at first glance. Her face was red from exertion, red from the burning rays of the noonday sun. There was sweat on her forehead that accumulated and ran into her eyes and down across her dusty cheeks, making streaks that added to her already unkempt appearance.

Her hair was tangled, but she didn't care. Her feet burned and ached in the high-button shoes that were nearly worn out now but had not been so when she left her ruined home. Her skirt was torn in half a dozen places. Because it was, it kept tripping her and making her fall.

For a while, she had looked behind at regular intervals, fearfully, as though waiting for pursuit. Now she didn't seem to care. Her face stayed straight

1

ahead, holding a certain exhausted fatalism it had never held before. If they caught her, they caught her. She would die. But if God was willing, they would not find her trail and she would go on, to the only place she knew to go—her nearest neighbor, forty miles away.

On and on, while the sun traveled with deliberate indifference across the brassy sky.

Those who lived out here knew this land—perhaps they admired its harsh and awesome beauty. They respected it, or feared it, or hated it. But they never loved it, because love is a gentle emotion and there was never anything gentle about this land.

In summer, its sun was pitiless, drying what little water was to be found, scorching everything that was unprotected from its searing glare. In winter northers whirled out of the far reaches of timbered high country to northward, which the girl had heard about but never seen. And snow, crusted with ice, hid the grass from hungry stock.

She knew nothing else. Her father had come here in 1850. The first sky her baby eyes had beheld had been the one above her; the first land her baby feet had trod had been the land beneath her now.

She stopped at sundown and found herself a small well of coolness in the lee of a towering sandstone rock. She lay down, but did not sleep. She only stared up at the changing colors in the sky, unseeing. There were pictures in her mind that she knew might fade with time but would never completely go away.

The picture of her father standing before the door last night, staring out across the land, seeing nothing but feeling danger with a sense as old as time itself. The picture of his worried face as they ate their supper in semi-darkness because he did not want them to light the lamps.

The picture glimpsed from one of the high, narrow rifle ports in the adobe walls of the house—a Comanche's painted, fiercely wild-eyed face only inches away from hers.

And sounds. Their high, staccato, barking shouts. The roar of her father's gun and of the one she held in her own brown hands.

And the feel of things—the cold, damp air of the narrow, moldy tunnel her father had dug and timbered long years ago for just a time as this. She'd crawled through there as a baby, learning not to be afraid of it. A part of her teaching had been that when her father said, "Get in the tunnel," she did so unhesitatingly, with neither question or protest. And so, this morning, when the order finally came, she unquestioningly obeyed.

The tunnel wound away from the house, and up, a monumental undertaking for one man and a task that had taken, in all, several years to complete. Away and up, for a quarter mile, to end beneath as enormous rock and emerge scarcely larger than a badger hole on the side of the rock that faced away from the house.

A monumental task, but it had saved the life he had meant for it to save.

She crawled through as she had done so many times before, knowing each turn and irregularity, knowing each timber by its feel beneath her hands. She came out into the first pink rays of the rising sun and looked back once from around the side of the enormous rock.

The house was burning inside and in the brush and sod thatching on the roof. Personal effects and furniture were piled in the yard and flaming high. Two white and naked bodies lay sprawled grotesquely in the yard—white, but blackened, too, and red in spots. There were other bodies, those of Comanches her father had killed before he was rushed and overcome.

And then she turned and ran.

Now, at nightfall, in the blessed coolness that comes with the passing of the sun, she rested in the lee of a great rock. She grieved, hated, felt uncertainty and fear.

She knew nothing but this land and therefore she would stay. Toward that end she would plan her actions and her life. But first she must reach the house of her neighbor, forty miles away.

A little rest, then on again to water at Arroyo Negro, twelve miles away from the ruined house. More rest and on again. At dawn, she had covered twenty miles.

On the ensuing day, she traveled fewer miles and rested more. Sunset found her with yet eleven miles to go.

She would reach the place by early dawn. Then she could rest; she could eat. And she could feel less terribly alone.

Owen Scobey was a comparative newcomer to the land. His house showed it—its newness was apparent. But it showed something else as well—he was here to stay.

It nestled against the side of a hill, half buried in the hill itself. Its walls were of adobe, three feet thick at their base. Its roof was beamed with twelve-inch logs, upon which a layer of closely laid poles rested, none of which were less than six inches at their butt ends. Over these was a layer of brush and over that a two-foot covering of dirt, which even the short years had sodded solidly on top. You could drive a team out on that roof and never know you were on anything less solid than virgin ground.

There was no cover closer than a hundred yards from the house—no place that would shelter a dark-skinned rifleman. The corral, the adobe barn, both were nearly two hundred yards away.

This day began like any other day. He awoke half an hour before dawn; he pumped water from the well that had been dug before the house was built and was now enclosed by it. He drank, then washed, then went and stirred the shoulder of the boy sleeping on the cot across the room from his own. "Matt. Come on."

He returned to the kitchen and built a fire in the fireplace. He put water on to heat.

By then, gray was touching the eastern sky and the boy was up. Scobey opened the door and, rifle in hand, stepped out onto the packed-dirt gallery. The boy, also holding a rifle, stepped out immediately behind.

Scobey was a tall and quiet-faced man, dark of skin, very blue of eye. His hair, while not yet thinning, was beginning to gray over his ears.

You'd have placed his age at forty, but you would have been wrong. He was thirty-two.

Something—some instinctive unease—made him say before he left the shadow of the overhanging roof, "Stay here, Matt."

Matt didn't speak. He was tall for twelve, thin and stringy, so that nothing ever fit him very well. His hair was long, showing signs of having occasionally hacked off with scissors. A quiet-faced boy, he looked at Scobey with some elusive quality in his grayish eyes compounded of unquestioning faith, respect, liking. . . .

Looking back as he stepped away, Owen Scobey felt, as always when Matt looked at him that way, the icy clutch of the hand of fear. God grant the boy never found him out. . . .

Five years now. Five years of this same cold fear. He'd hidden himself and the boy deliberately out here, where only Indians ever came.

Give him a few more years. Give him ten, he thought. The boy would be twenty-two. Maybe then he'd be able to understand. . . .

Scobey crossed the yard watchfully. He carried his rifle at arm's length with seeming negligence, but he could have snapped it to his shoulder and fired in the smallest part of a second.

The sky grew lighter rapidly, noticeably changing even as he crossed the yard. The plain lay open and empty on all sides, grass waving very lightly in the early-morning breeze. It could conceal half a hundred painted plains warriors, he knew. And maybe it did, for he seldom felt this crawling unease without there being good reason for it.

The figure he saw stumble over a distant rise and approach was not a Comanche but could be part of a Comanche trap.

He glanced over his shoulder, then backed watchfully toward the house. His throat felt dry; his chest felt tight.

You lived with this fear out here. You accepted it as part of the conditions of staying. In some it dulled, until they began to ignore its constant threat. And those in whom it dulled were the ones that died.

It hadn't dulled in Owen. It never would. Someone with others to protect—if he loved them—could never fail to feel its sharpened edge every hour of every day.

As he reached the gallery overhang, the boy whispered, "Comanche?"

"Don't know. Keep still."

They watched the figure stumble on. Matt said, "She's white!"

"Maybe. Looks so. We'll wait and see."

The Comanches were sly. They didn't favor dying any more than anybody else. They'd not risk losing half their number in an open attack if they could do it any other way. Like releasing a captive within sight of a white man's house, and cutting him off from his house when he ran heedlessly out to help.

The woman was closer now. He could see her burned and dusty face. He could see her ragged clothes and sometimes one of her worn-out shoes. But not until she was less than three hundred yards away did he move from the sheltering overhang of the roof.

Then he said shortly, "Keep still. I'll get her," and he walked away.

She stopped momentarily when she saw him. Froze and stared and then came on. She stumbled and fell and did not get up.

Scobey reached her. But before he stooped to gather her up, he looked long and carefully at the empty land around him. Then he lifted her and carried her at a swift walk back toward the house.

Matt held the door for him and he carried her inside. He laid her down on his own bed after Matt had smoothed the covers for him.

Two males—man and boy—staring down helplessly and not knowing what to do. Matt said in a hushed voice, as though the girl could hear, "Is she hurt, Mr. Scobey?"

"Don't know." Owen stooped awkwardly and removed her shoes one by one. "Feet's bloody, but that's from walkin'. Get a pan of water and a towel."

The boy went out. Scobey heard the handle of the pump.

His face burning with embarrassment, he looked the girl over carefully, seeking blood on her clothing. He turned her over gingerly and inspected her back similarly. He sighed almost inaudibly with relief.

Matt came in with the pan and towel. Scobey swung her legs over the edge of the bed and immersed her feet in the water. He said, "Hold the pan," and while Matt did, he washed the crusted blood and prairie earth from her feet. He dried them and replaced them on the bed.

He said gruffly, "Come on. Now she needs a lot of sleep. She's come a long ways."

"You know her, Mr. Scobey?"

"No. But she must be that young'un of Will Pryor's. Seems he said his girl was about this age."

Matt's face was pale and his eyes glanced warily toward the barred outside door. Scobey nodded. "I reckon, boy. She wouldn't be out wanderin' around alone if her folks were still alive."

"You think they'll be coming here?"

Scobey shrugged. "Nobody knows what a Comanche will do. Might be just one raid. Might be they're three hundred miles away by now."

Matt's eyes were steady for all his face was pale. "Might be they're three hundred yards, too."

Scobey nodded. "We'll be careful."

He glanced at the girl once more, at her cruelly sunburned face, at the matted tangle of her hair. Then he went out and closed the door of the tiny room behind.

He crossed to the rifle port and stared outside.

The sun was started on its journey up and across the sky. Heat waves rose shimmering from the baked and bare expanse of yard. He wondered how the girl had got away. Seemed impossible, but there it was.

He glanced toward Matt Conger. He felt a cold and sudden stab of fear. Premonition was needling him but it was so vague that he could not pin it down.

Of one thing he was sure. The girl would change their life whether they liked it or not. She would have to be got out and he couldn't leave young Matt alone.

Therein, he supposed, lay the danger and his fear. Settlements meant people. A lot of people. Maybe some that knew. Maybe one that would tell.

If he only had a few more years. But he wouldn't have. Hiding out here had been the act of a fool. Inevitably, no matter what, the truth would seek him out.

☆ 2 ☆

THEY watched all day, but nothing moved anywhere within range of their vision. And in late afternoon, Scobey went out to tend his horses, the two he kept up for his own and Matt's use.

Matt stood with his rifle beneath the overhang of the roof. Owen carried his with him while he led the horses to the dry stream bed. He let them drink from a hole he had dug there after the last water came down several months before. Fed by an underground flow, it was four feet across, three deep, and green with algae and moss.

When they had drank their fill, he led them back. He forked hay to them, hay cut from the prairie and hauled here to the haystack standing idle behind the barn. Then he returned to the house.

Matt Conger went in and Scobey followed. The girl stood in the doorway of the bedroom.

She put her hands to her hair, smoothing it ineffectually. There was haunted memory in her eyes, but there was something else as well. Determination. Even anger.

Scobey asked, "You Pryor's girl?"

She nodded.

"Is he—and your ma—was it Comanches?"

She nodded again numbly.

"How'd you get away?"

"The tunnel. He dug it a long time ago." Her voice was cracked and hoarse, but it was the first woman's voice Owen had heard for more than a year.

He said, "Hungry?"

She nodded.

"Then sit down and eat. It's ready."

He turned his back on her and crossed to the fireplace. He began to set out the meal—beans, coffee made from roasted beans, fresh antelope stew.

She ate greedily, occasionally glancing up at either Scobey or Matt with a kind of shamed apology in her eyes. Apology for eating thus. Apology for being able to eat at all when her parents lay mutilated and dead only forty miles away.

But life went on. She was a healthy, hardy girl or she'd never have made it across those forty blistering miles. The demands of the flesh were strong. . . .

Scobey and Matt sat down and ate with her. There was little talk.

When she had finished, Scobey said, "Matt, that pair of shoes you outgrew a year ago—they still around?"

"Uh huh."

"Get 'em. And a pair of clean socks."

He glanced at the girl. "Likely they won't fit to well. They'll hurt for a time. But they'll be better than no shoes at all."

"I'm obliged."

Matt brought her the shoes and socks. She bent and began to put them on.

"What's your name?"

"Kathleen. Kathleen Pryor. Pa called me Kate."

He saw that her eyes misted and said quickly, "Then we will, too. You got folks someplace?"

She shook her head.

"None at all?" An odd dismay touched him.

Again she shook her head.

"You can't stay here."

"No, I don't suppose I can."

"I don't mean—well, hell, you're welcome enough—it's just—"

"It's all right, Mr. Scobey. I understand."

Owen mumbled, "Ain't proper, that's all."

She said firmly, "I'm going back, anyway."

Owen got up abruptly and paced to one of the rifle ports. His eye had caught movement out there on the plain in the direction from which the girl had come. Vague movement and sudden, upon which his eyes instantly focused. But too late. He could not have said whether it was Comanche, or bird, or small animal. It was movement and that was all.

Silently he watched. He saw nothing else, no motion in the waving grass.

Matt got up from the table and started for the door. Scobey asked, "Where you going?"

"I was cleaning out the barn. I—"

"Let it go today."

Matt's eyes sharpened and rested for a lengthened moment on Scobey's face. Owen went to the stove, got the coffeepot and refilled his own and Kathleen's cup.

Kate said, "Did you see something?"

"Don't know. Maybe just thought I did."

Kate's voice was frightened. "They're here. Pa— He felt them, too, before he ever saw a thing."

"Maybe. We'll stay inside."

"Can they—"

"They won't get in and they can't burn the house. We've got water and food. We can wait 'em out."

That wasn't strictly true. It depended on how badly the Indians wanted the inhabitants of the house; on how much they were willing to pay to get them.

He said, "What do you mean, you're going back? You haven't even got a house to go to."

Her eyes showed him anger and then stubbornness. "I'm still going back."

He shrugged. She'd get over that. She'd realize how impossible it was.

She said angrily, "My father spent his life here and so have I. Five thousand cattle wear his Spanish Spur. But money? What little gold he had is buried in the ashes of the house."

"You could sell, couldn't you?"

"Maybe. If I could find a buyer. And if I'd sell for two cents on the dollar."

Scobey shook his head. Nobody would buy. Not in the middle of a Comanche uprising. But for a girl to stay out here alone was unthinkable.

His irritation grew. Damn her, she knew how impossible it was. He wondered if he was going to have to haul her out of the country by force.

Matt finished his coffee, got up silently and went to one of the rifle ports. He put the point of his shoulder comfortably against the adobe wall and stared outside. Scobey watched him with brooding eyes.

Matt had been seven when Owen took him. Owen had lived that day over a hundred times in the ensuing five year and in spite of himself, he lived it over again right now.

A lousy mistake—mistake on Owen's part—mistake on the part of Dave Conger.

You rode into a strange town, hardly a town because it was nothing more than a stage depot that was both restaurant and saloon, half a dozen houses and a trading post. Looking for Dave Conger and carrying a warrant charging him with murder.

A strange frontier town whose inhabitants were mostly men with warrants of one kind or another out for them someplace. Men who carried guns and who protected each other with outlaw clannishness.

Because they were the way they were, Owen had been a bit on the nervous side. Too ready with his gun. Too quick to shoot.

Conger was in the stage depot, standing at the bar. There could be no mistake about who he was—Owen had seen him briefly half a dozen times during the long, long chase.

Standing at the bar with his back to the door. Owen had called to him to drop his gun and belt; instead, Conger had whirled.

Maybe not reaching for his gun. Owen would never know. Being nervous—perhaps a bit too quick himself—Owen had simply assumed he was.

It was painful to remember because there was an uneasy feeling in the depths of this man that he had killed unnecessarily.

He'd drawn his gun and shot. Not to kill, in spite of the rushed tension of the moment. To cripple. But Conger had been moving too fast for a sure crippling shot. He'd caught it squarely in the chest. And his hand had never touched his gun.

Owen frowned now and stared at the empty land beyond the rifle port. Had Conger been reaching for his gun or had he been extending his hands preparatory to raising them in surrender? Those in the stage depot swore he had been surrendering. They swore Owen murdered him.

And the boy—Conger's son—sleeping at the time of the shooting in one of the tiny depot rooms. He couldn't stay. Not there. No one wanted him or indeed was even equipped to care for him.

Mistakes. Stupid, unnecessary mistakes. Like the one attacked and murdered his wife only to discover he'd killed an innocent man. Hence, the murder warrant. Hence, the flight westward, taking the boy. Conger had been making for California and hoping for a fresh start there.

So Owen Scobey took the boy and started east with him.

On the way, he thought of what lay ahead of young Matt because of what he had done. An orphanage. Maybe being farmed out to someone who would want him only because of the work he could perform.

Sickened of his lawman's star, guilty, driven partly by selfishness, partly by selflessness, Owen turned aside and headed south. He'd keep the boy. He'd try to undo the wrong he suspected he had committed. And by so doing, by trying to make up to Matt for the death of his father, he might ease the crawling guilt in his own uneasy mind.

Again something moved out there on the plain and this time Owen caught a glimpse of feathers and copper skin and bright war paint. But he didn't move. He didn't turn his head and he didn't speak, too caught up in the past to care much about Comanches slipping up on the house. He'd grown to love young Matt as he would have loved his own small son. And with his love had come his fear— that Matt would find him out. That the boy's respect and love for him would turn to hate.

Outside, they were growing bolder. An Indian

brave left the shelter of high grass and sprinted for the cover of the barn.

Owen jerked his rifle up, drew his bead, snapped the rifle ahead slightly to lead the man. He fired.

The Indian pitched forward, stumbling, as the bullet struck. He fell sprawling, jerked a couple of times and laid still.

Matt yelped, "You got him!" in a high, excited voice. There was no fear in that young voice. Not yet. But there was fear in Owen. He knew their fortress was not as impregnable as he had led the others to believe. Nothing had ever been built that could resist prolonged and determined attack. The front door was only wood. It could be battered in or burned.

He swung his head briefly. The girl, Kate, stood in the center of the room. Her face was white and she was trembling. Her eyes were plainly seeing the sights of the other attack, culminating with the last view she'd had of the house. And there was no tunnel here.

Owen's glance was brief. Then he stared back out at the plain. There was only one way in which the Comanches could be driven off. Their attack must be made so costly that they would give it up.

Owen said, "Shoot at everything that moves, Matt."

"All right, Mr. Scobey."

"And don't miss."

"I won't, Mr. Scobey."

He wouldn't either. For twelve—for any age—the boy was good. Owen had been teaching him to shoot almost since the time he'd taken him.

He heard Kate's voice from the center of the room. "Have you got another gun?"

"Over in the corner beside the fireplace. Know how to load a muzzle-loader?"

"I know."

"Powder, ball, and caps are in a box beside the gun. Put 'em out on the table. Loading every one, you won't get many shots. So make 'em count."

"I will, Mr. Scobey."

Owen watched. He saw a feather rise and move out in the high grass beyond the barn. He heard Matt's rifle bark and there was a thrashing in the grass. Then all was still again.

Minutes dragged past. Kate got the rifle loaded and took her place at a rifle port on Scobey's left. He said, "Don't show any more of yourself than you have to. Some of the bucks are pretty good."

He didn't fear the day. But he did fear the coming night. It was then that the Indians would be able to approach the house closely. It was then that they'd make their try at burning the house or battering in the door.

They didn't like to fight at night—some superstition about the soul of a warrior killed at night. But that didn't mean they wouldn't fight in the darkness if they had to.

He shot a glance at Matt. The boy was like a statue, like a boy watching a rabbit hole. It was a game to him. A game so far.

Matt felt Owen's glance upon him and swung his head. He grinned nervously.

Owen returned the grin reassuringly. Then he put his attention back on the land outside.

He was a fool, he guessed. A fool to fear so much. There had not been over fifty men in that settlement the day he'd killed Matt's father. Fifty men scattered now over a million square miles of frontier country. Fifty men, who lived by violence, some of whom would surely be dead by now.

Fear the present—the painted braves outside the house. Let the future take care of itself.

But the core of unease in the pit of his belly would not go away.

☆ 3 ☆

THE sun sank toward the western horizon behind the house with implacable relentlessness. It set, and stained the scattered clouds a brilliant orange that faded to pink, to purple, and finally to a dingy gray.

Shadows now lay upon the land and visibility was reduced. Counting on reduced visibility, the Indians began to slink toward the adobe barn.

One, more bold than the others, made his run openly. Owen, Matt and Kate fired almost simultaneously. The brave dropped without a sound, without further movement after he hit the ground. But the others reached the place.

There was a period during which nothing happened, during which the light steadily faded until Owen could scarcely see the barn itself. Then he heard the Indians' guttural talk. He heard a horse nicker shrilly. And he cursed softly under his breath.

They had the horses. They had his and Matt's mounts. Even if they were driven off, he and Matt were afoot.

He swung his head and spoke toward Kate. "Think you could fix something to eat in the dark?"

"If you'll tell me where things are." Her voice was soft, scared, but steady for all of that. And

19

pleasant. A woman's voice, welcome after five years of living alone with Matt.

He said, "Bread is in a bin to the right of the fireplace. Molasses in a can on the shelf over the bin. Spread some butter on it and pump some water. We'll do our cooking and eat our hot meals when it's light."

He thought wryly that they might well never see the light again. Except briefly, perhaps, at dawn when the Indians massed and attacked through a door they had burned out during the night.

That was the way he'd work it if he were one of the Indian braves instead of their intended prey. And that was probably the way they'd work it too.

He said, "Go ahead and eat something, boy. Nothing to shoot at now."

He heard Matt pull away from the aperture and cross the room. He heard the sounds Kate made— that of the bread bin being opened, that of the molasses can being withdrawn from the shelf. Familiar sounds, heard a thousand times.

His mind returned to Matt. The boy had never had a chance to be a boy, he thought. Not really. And that explained, perhaps, why Matt was so grown up for twelve. Quiet. Thoughtful. A man already.

He could shoot. Owen felt sure pressure wouldn't panic him. Between them, they'd make this place costly for the savages even if they lost out in the end.

And that girl. She'd get her chance at dawn to even the score for her murdered folks.

He heard a rustle beside him and her voice. "Here's some bread and a dipper of water."

He leaned the gun against the wall. He groped for the food, found it and began to eat.

She said, "Why couldn't our cattle be driven north?"

He said, "They could."

"Father said there had been some drives made to Kansas. Not from here—from father south and east. He heard cattle were bringing from twelve to twenty dollars a head."

"Could be. I don't know."

She spoke, almost as though to herself. "A thousand head at twelve dollars. That's twelve thousand dollars. If I had that I could hire men. I could rebuild our house. I could stay."

Owen said, "Takes men to gather cattle. Takes men to make a drive. Takes money to hire men."

"But if I promised them a share . . ."

Her voice was softly presistent. He felt a certain irritation, and fought it down. She had lost her home. She had lost her family. She was completely and terribly alone, homeless, and yet she had this grit. She was planning ahead instead of whining for a man to fish her out of her predicament.

He said with enforced patience, "Comanches. Those outside right now. It would take an army to gather your herd, an army to drive them north."

He heard her sigh softly as though in defeat. But her voice, even though conceding defeat, contained more in its tone. "I suppose you're right."

There was silence while Owen finished his bread and drained the dipper. Then her voice, soft and scarcely distinguishable. "He dug that tunnel to save my life. He fought and held them back while I escaped. His whole life was for mother and for me. I won't let it go for nothing. I won't let it be lost!"

Owen said, "Go get some sleep. You'll wake up if anything starts happening."

He knew how it would start. There would be

sounds out there at the barn as they tore the combustibles loose. Then more furtive sounds as they slipped through the darkness, carrying them to the house and piling them in front of the door. Maybe he'd get a few of them, but he wouldn't get them all. Not shooting in the dark.

Then there'd be rustling sounds as the stuffed dry grass beneath and around the boards. And maybe he'd get a shot or two as they touched it off.

He listened. He heard a sharp crack out at the barn, followed by the screech of a nail torn loose. They were starting. They were doing what he had expected of them.

He strained his eyes, gun held ready and steadied against the side of the aperture. Apparently they were prepared to lose as many men as necessary to take this place. And that was strange. Usually Comanches—any Plains Indian for that matter—fought only as long as the battle was going well. When their losses got too high, they concluded that the signs were unfavorable, that luck was against them, and withdrew. But not this bunch. They had lost three already, with nothing gained. They would lose at least half a dozen more when they rushed the place at dawn.

Owen could think of but two possible reasons for their recklessness. Either they wanted Kate badly enough to take any risk, or there was help for the besieged whites on the way, and close.

He heard the scrape of something against the ground outside. Damn! There weren't even any stars tonight. Clouds must have spread across the sky. And he couldn't see a thing.

He waited. It was like listening to the rustling of mice in a dark and silent room. You could hear but you couldn't see.

He felt something beside him, assumed it was Matt, started slightly when Kate spoke softly right beside him. "There's not much chance, is there? No more than father and mother had."

He said gruffly, "I wouldn't say that. They'll burn the door. Or try. If we keep throwing water on it, maybe we can keep it from burning through. If the door's still standing at dawn, they'll have to wait another day."

"They can wait."

"Maybe. But he wasn't sure. They weren't acting as though they had all the time in the world.

The girl asked, "Is he your son?"

"I'm raisin' him." There was plain hostility in his tone.

"I didn't mean to pry. I'm sorry."

"Forget it."

"Will you help me make that drive—to Kansas, I mean?'"

"No. And neither will anybody else."

He snapped his rifle up and fired, quickly and without thought, at a shadow dimly seen less than ten yards away. There was a yelp of pain, a brief flurry of motion, and silence again.

Another wait. Matt was silent at the other aperture. Right now it looked as though there was little danger of Matt's ever finding him out. It didn't look as though they had that long to live.

He wished he could get Matt out. But he knew he couldn't. He hadn't had the foresight Pryor possessed. He hadn't dug a tunnel leading away from the house.

The girl murmered, "You don't have to be so unpleasant about it."

"I'm sorry. Only, you've got to face the facts. Nobody can drive cattle or even gather them as long as the tribes are all stirred up. Best thing you can do is go down to Fort Worth and wait. Sooner or later, the Army will send out some cavalry and drive the Indians north."

"And what do you suggest I live on while I'm there?"

He said sourly, "You might try working. There are people that do."

"I don't think I like you, Mr. Scobey."

"Ain't necessary that you do."

"What are you hiding? There's something. . . ."

Suddenly his voice was angry. "Maybe there is. Whatever it is, it's none of your damn business. That plain enough?"

"Yes. That's plain enough."

She moved away, leaving him ashamed, and angry because he was. She went across to the other aperture and he heard her talking softly to Matt. He growled, "All that noise sure gives the redskins a dandy target to shoot at."

Matt said, "You were . . ." and subsided without finishing. But his young voice had been touched with defiance, and Scobey knew he had been wrong.

He could sympathize with Kate's loss, with the awful feeling of abandonment and aloneness she must be experiencing. He could sympathize with her determination to save something of what her father had spent his life building. But he couldn't sympathize with her stubbornness. What she had suggested was impossible, only she wouldn't admit that it was.

He examined himself honestly, realizing that the turmoil in his own thoughts was largely responsible for his irritation with her. She was a strong-bodied womanly girl and Owen had been long without a woman. That had entered his thoughts, however fleetingly. Also contributing was his own sense of guilt and fear. He wanted more time with Matt.

The hours slipped away. Kate left Matt and crossed the room. A homemade, rawhide-covered chair creaked as she sat down.

Outside, the furtive noise continued. And the pile of wood and grass against the door grew steadily in size. Owen said, "Matt, go get some sleep."

"I—"

"Go get some sleep, boy."

"All right, Mr. Scobey."

He glanced across the pitch-dark room. "You get some too, girl."

"My name's Kate."

"All right, Kate. Get some sleep. And—well, hell, I'm sorry."

"Does that mean—"

"It doesn't mean a thing. Just that I'm sorry."

He sat there afterward, staring sourly, angrily out at the night. He wished he had constructed these rifle ports so that they commanded a view of the door. But he hadn't and there was nothing he could do about it now.

Suddenly light flared outside and he understood at once the cause of it. The Indians had lighted the dry grass they had piled against the door.

He knew they carried no matches—indeed, seldom could obtain them. But he also knew that they sometimes carried live coals with them in containers lined with mud.

The light grew rapidly and he stood tense and ready, waiting for a shot. He got none. Rifles flared and barked from the direction of the barn and bullets thudded against the adobe walls of the house. One skinned the side of the rifle port and showered him with stinging dust.

He ducked aside. Kate and Matt were visible to him now in the light that filtered through the narrow rifle ports. He said, "Pump some water. Fill everything you can find—buckets, pans. Set 'em by the door."

No use now in standing ready at the apertures. No Indians would show themselves in the light outside. Not much use in soaking the inside of the door, either. Not enough water would soak through to protect it from the flames. But there was another way. . . .

Matt worked the pump handle steadily while Kate held receptacles under the spout. Scobey took them from her and carried them to the door, where he set them all down handily.

Ten minutes later, every receptacle in the house that would hold water was full and waiting. Owen said, "Each of you take a rifle port. Keep down as low as you can. Shoot at gun flashes, because that's all you're going to see."

Matt asked, "What are you going to do?"

"Open the door. Douse that fire."

"You'll get—Mr. Scobey, don't!"

"Get over to the rifle port." Scobey shot the heavy bar back and flung open the door. He seized the largest bucket and flung its contents through and onto the searing, crackling flames. He flung it aside, seized another and emptied it similarly. They seemed to have no immediate effect other than to raise huge showers of sparks and steam. He worked frantically, as rapidly as he could, paying no attention to the bullets that buzzed through the door, that tore into the doorjamb and into the adobe walls to each side of it.

He made a good target, he knew—lighted by the

flames, against the dark background of the interior of the house.

But he was doing some good. The flames were lessening as he worked and as he neared the end of the filled receptacles, died out altogether.

He stopped immediately, flung a last bucket over the outside surface of the door and tried to slam it shut. It caught on debris, and he worked like a madman to free it.

He heard the yells of Comanches as they charged. He heard shots coming regularly from the gun ports inside the house. He knew he'd never clear the door in time. A heavy timber was wedged in the doorway and refused to budge. By the time he got it loose, they'd be on him and inside. . . .

He gave up and snatched his rifle, which was leaning against the wall not far from the door. He jumped back and waited for the first of the Indians to come charging through the door.

Instead, he heard the rapid thunder of many hoofs, the high yells of men, the barking of long-barreled revolvers and, unbelievably, a bugle sounding the charge.

He waited, and didn't relax at all. This could be another Comanche trick. In a few minutes, he would know.

☆ 4 ☆

A WELCOME sound was the shout "Hello the house! You all right in there?"

There was still shooting, but it was diminishing with distance. Scobey stepped through the door, picking his way over the smoldering debris that had been piled against it. Too dark to see. But he could make out the shapes of horses and their riders and he could hear the unmistakable rattle of accouterments, the chain-of-command orders passing from officers to noncoms to enlisted men.

He called, "All right, Captain. All right." The horizan in the east was visible now. The sky was charcoal gray, the land beneath it black.

The voice again, "Anybody hurt here?"

"Nobody hurt, Captain."

"Who are you?"

"Owen Scobey. Matt Conger. Kate Pryor. She's the daughter of Will Pryor, over east of here."

"We came past there." The voice spoke more softly. "Nothing much left. We buried her folks. How the devil did she get away?"

"Tunnel."

The sky was turning lighter. Scobey could now see the man to whom he spoke—tall, dusty, lean as

28

rawhide, mustached and bewhiskered. He could see the others behind the captain—a burial detail removing the bodies of the dead Indians, others building small cooking fires. Behind him, Matt and Kate came through the door and stood uncertainly in the cold, gray morning light.

Scobey said, "Kate Pryor, Captain. And Matt."

The captain dismounted, sweeping off his hat. "Richards, ma'am. And I'm pleased. We camped a few miles south of here and our sentries heard the shots."

Kate didn't speak.

The captain stared at her closely. "We'll escort you out, of course, ma'am."

"No, thank you, Captain. I'll stay."

The captain glanced at Owen, then back to Kate. His voice was tolerant, sympathetic. "We'll talk of it later, ma'am."

Kate didn't reply. Owen glanced at her face. It was determined, almost cold. She picked up her tattered skirt and turned. "I'll fix something to eat."

Owen said, "Join us, Captain?"

"I'll eat with my men, thank you. Our rations— You wouldn't have a bit of sugar to spare, would you?"

"Of course. Matt—"

The captain called. "Delehanty! Accompany this young man."

Matt followed Kate into the house. The corporal followed Matt. He emerged a few minutes later, carrying a large lard can filled with sugar.

It was light now, light enough to see clearly. There were about thirty troopers in the yard. Owen asked, "How many men do you have, Captain?"

"Two lieutenants and a hundred and forty-eight

men. Three scouts and a tracker. Come with me, Mr. Scobey. I'll introduce you."

Owen walked beside him. A trooper came and took the captain's horse.

The men had several fires going already. They were cooking bacon and heating water for tea. They were an exhausted-looking bunch, and most of them did not even bother to glance up.

Owen asked, "How long have you been out, Captain?"

"Three weeks tomorrow. Our supply wagons are well behind us and we need some rest. The damned Comanches won't let us get it."

"Can't catch 'em, huh?"

"Oh, we've caught them, all right. Where they want us to. We've had two skirmishes with them. Both times, they withdrew as soon as we began to get the best of them. But we're driving them north and that's what we came out to do."

At a separate fire just ahead, Owen saw four men. One wore a cavalry uniform and a second-lieutenant's bar. Richards said, "Lieutenant Mills—Mr. Scobey."

Scobey shook hands with the young man, who appeared very tired and very green. He glanced toward the other three.

His eyes touched the tracker as Richards said, "Jesus Chavez, our tracker." The dark-skinned, dark-haired man neither rose nor offered to shake hands, so Owen only nodded.

Richards said, "Mr. Quade. Mr. Leo Quade, one of our scouts."

Quade was as old as ancient parchment and as dry. His eyes, pale and blue, were surrounded with tiny wrinkles in his leathery skin. Most of his teeth were gone, but there was a sharpness, an alertness about him that belied his age. He shook hands with Scobey, nodded and said, "I'll be goin', Cap'n. I want to ketch McGee afore sunup."

Richard nodded. Quade shuffled away toward his waiting horse.

Owen glanced at the third man, who until now had presented only his back to them.

There was something very hollow, very empty in Owen's belly as he watched the man turn. He scarcely heard Richards' voice. "This is Beecher Tilton, one of our other scouts."

Tilton was grinning faintly. He extended his hand. "Glad to know you, Scobey."

"The same." Owen took Tilton's hand, shook it briefly and released it. Tilton said, "Grub's hot, Cap'n."

"Thank you, Mr. Tilton."

Owen turned and strode away. After he had gone ten yards, he swung his head and looked around. Tilton was watching him, that faint grin still on his bony face.

He was a tall man, thin and slightly stooped. But wiry. He had not shaved for several days. His skin was as dark as that of Chavez, the tracker. Owen turned his head and continued toward the house, Tilton's image plain and indelible before his eyes.

You didn't forget a man like Beecher Tilton, because he was as individualistic in his way as Captain Richards was. He wore a gun, sagging against his dusty thigh and tied above the knee. Holster and belt were stained and stiff with sweat and dust. But the gun was oiled and smooth and as deadly as a rattler's fang.

Neither did you forget Beecher Tilton's face or eyes. There were both arrogance and cruelty written there. The Tiltons marched across the reaches of frontier, taking what they pleased and killing whoever dared stand in their way. A product of the times, of the code that proclaimed and protected every man's right to defend himself.

But Owen Scobey had another reason for remembering Beecher Tilton. Tilton had been present in the tiny stage depot the day Scobey shot and killed Dave Conger five years ago.

Fifty men. A million square miles to lose them in. And Tilton had to show up here. Scobey cursed softly under his breath. He stepped into the house.

He was greeted by the smell of frying meat, of baking biscuits, of real coffee brewing. Kate showed him a timid smile. "The trooper brought it in exchange for the sugar."

"Kind of him." He watched her closely, puzzled and disturbed by some new quality evident in her face.

She had combed and brushed her hair. She had brushed her dress and pinned the worst rips in it. There was color in her cheeks, the color of excitement, he supposed. But there was also a strange brightness in her eyes that made him vaguely uneasy.

He sat down and began to eat. Matt asked, "Can we go with 'em a ways, Mr. Scobey?"

"No, boy. But we'll go far enough to catch us up some mounts."

Kate went to the door and stepped outside. He couldn't blame her for her interest in the men, he supposed. A girl must lead a mighty lonely life out here.

He finished hurriedly, got up and wandered to the door. Kate was surrounded by troopers, talking, fifty yards from the house. As he watched, she left them and wandered on, toward the fire around which were grouped Richards, Lieutenant Mills, Chavez and Tilton.

Scobey scowled. He watched her still as she approached the fire. Richards and Mills stood up courteously. Chavez, the tracker, glanced up briefly and then returned his attention to his food. Tilton lounged easily, waiting to be introduced.

She shook his hand briefly, talked to him several moments, then turned away. Tilton kept pace with her. The two stopped ten or fifteen yards from the fire and talked. Then Kate left him and returned hurriedly toward the house.

The excitement he had seen previously in her eyes was stronger now. She said breathlessly, "Mr. Scobey, we've got some help!"

"Help for what?"

"To drive my father's cattle north! Mr. Tilton has promised to help. He says he thinks the other scout—Mr. Quade—will help, and probably the tracker, too. Se says now that Captain Richards has caught up with the Comanches, he won't have need for more then one scout."

"What'd you promise him?" There was a cold kind of dread in Owen. That which he feared most had happened. For all Tilton's pretense of not knowing him, he knew that the man remembered him well enough.

"A share."

"How much?"

"Ten per cent."

Owen groaned helplessly.

She didn't seem to notice. "He says gathering a herd will be easy now that Captain Richards has the Comanches on the run. He said to offer you ten per cent, but give the others only five."

"Generous of him," Owen said dryly.

For the first time, her enthusiasm dimmed. She looked up at him pleadingly. "What else could I do? I have no money to hire men."

Owen stared across the room at Matt, at the boy who had never had a chance to be a boy. He had the feeling that before this drive was finished, Matt would know.

And what then? Where would the boy go? Where could he go? He'd had enough hard blows, losing his mother, his home—losing his father. If he lost Owen this way . . .

Owen said, "I'll help you gather the herd, but I won't go north with you."

"Why?"

He stared at her almost angrily. "I have my own place here. I won't go off and leave it to the Indians."

Hostility between them verged on dislike. And yet as he looked at her, an aching kind of hunger touched him.

There was a knock on the open door and Scobey looked up to see Tilton standing there. The man stared briefly at him, then at Matt, and finally Kate. "I've spoken to the captain, Miss Pryor. He says it will be all right. He'll release me to help you with your drive. He'll also release Chavez and Quade."

He switched his glance to Owen. "You seem familiar, Mr. Scobey. Haven't we met someplace before?"

Owen couldn't help switching his glance to Matt, who was watching him with steady eyes. Owen felt something almost like physical pain in his chest. How soon would those young eyes hold hate as they looked at him? How soon?

He said, "Maybe. I don't know."

"Seems like I remember you. Scobey. Scobey. The name has a familiar sound."

Owen stared at him angrily. There was a taunting quality in Tilton's eyes.

Owen said, "I told Miss Pryor I'd help her gather her herd. But I won't go north with you."

Tilton's eyes narrowed. He said, "I hope you'll change your mind. You know cattle and you know the country. And without you, we'll be too few."

Owen didn't reply. The taunting quality in Tilton's eyes became more pronounced. "I keep trying to remember where I've seen you, Mr. Scobey. I hope you change your mind about accompanying the drive. I doubt if we can make it without your help. And if we don't, there's nothing in it either for us or for Miss Pryor, is there?"

Owen got up and walked outside. Kate stared after him, puzzlement in her eyes. Matt started to follow, but Owen said irritably, "Stay here, Matt. Stay here."

The boy looked hurt. Tilton grinned, then followed Scobey out. When they were beyond earshot of the house, Scobey stopped. "You remember me."

"Sure. I remember you. I've been watching the way you look at the boy—and the way he looks at you. You wouldn't want him to know you killed his pa."

Anger leaped in Owen. "I ought to kill you."

Tilton's eyes narrowed. Something entered them that was ugly and unpleasant, the look of an animal to whom killing is pleasure and a thing to be enjoyed. Tilton said softly, "Try, Mr. Scobey. You won't find me as easy as you found Dave Conger."

Owen clenched his fists. He could feel tremors of fury traveling through his body.

Tilton's voice was even, but deadly. "You'll help

us gather, Mr. Scobey, and you'll help us drive. Not that I want you along. But we'll need all the help we can get or we'll never get through, and I want that ten per cent."

"And if I don't?"

"Then I'll tell the boy who you are. I'll tell him what you've done."

Smiling, Tilton turned and walked away. Owen stared helplessly after him. An hour ago, or less, he had faced sure death behind the jammed and open door of the house. Now he faced something worse.

Before this was through, he would kill Tilton or be killed himself. But if he lived, he would be a different man than he was right now. He couldn't help but be, because there was nothing he wouldn't do to keep young Matt.

☆ 5 ☆

THE command pulled out at eight, taking the trail of the fleeing Indians. Tilton and Chavez remained behind, after volunteering to ride out and drive in Scobey's horse herd, which, he hoped, had not been driven off by the Comanches. They left at nine, were gone three hours, and returned just before noon, driving the herd of twenty-two horses ahead of them.

Owen was glumly sour, worried. Matt was excited at the prospect of the drive north to Kansas. Even Kate seemed changed. Rested, washed, dressed in clean but baggy and outsize clothing belonging to Owen, she was more animated and cheerful than he had seen her. Grief for her parents, and shock, still lingered in the depths of her eyes, but she kept herself under control, mostly by keeping very busy, cooking, cleaning, creating such a commotion that Owen and Matt were virtually forced to leave.

In midafternoon, Quade came riding in, dismounted and unsaddled his horse. He rubbed the horse down, put him into the corral with the others and watched him kick and bite his way to the pile of hay. Then he crossed the yard to where Owen was hunkered in the shade against the adobe wall of the

37

house. Over by the barn, Tilton and Matt sat, Matt apparently enthralled by some tall tale being told him by the lanky gun fighter.

Quade squinted at Owen with pale, sharp eyes. "Cap'n tells me you're figurin' on takin' a herd to Kansas."

Owen nodded.

"An' that your payin' five per cent of the herd to every man that helps."

"That's right, too. It's Miss Pryor's herd."

"You goin'?"

Owen nodded.

"An' Tilton an' Chavez, too, I reckon?"

Owen nodded again. Quade squinted at him closely. "You don't like it much, do you?"

"No." Owen didn't elaborate.

As though talking to himself, Quade said, "Chavez is a good man. He's half Comanche an' half Mexican. The Indian blood comes from his pa. Seems his ma was captured in a raid an' taken as a squaw by one of the Comanche bucks. She was rescued by the rangers, but she was already carryin' Chavez. She hated Comanches an' so does Chavez. Good tracker. He can foller sign like an Indian can."

Owen didn't speak. He was beginning to like Quade. The man must be seventy or more and it showed. But age hadn't slowed him down. He was still as tough as weathered rawhide.

Quade stared at Owen briefly with those pale, sharp eyes, then turned his head and spat his cud of tobacco on the ground. "Know this Tilton, do you?"

Owen shook his head.

A different, angry light in Quade's old eyes now. He fairly spat his words. "Killer! But good readin' sign an' good in a scrap. He can hit somethin' tossed in the air three times afore it hits the ground. He'll take the whole damn herd if he can."

Quade hunkered down comfortably beside Owen and rolled himself a smoke. "What you doin' it fer, anyhow?"

"The drive?" Owen frowned. "To get her a stake and get her off my hands, I guess. Indians killed her folks and burned her out. She's got no money and no place to go. If the drive comes off, she can rebuild her house and hire men to run the place."

"Takin' any of your own cattle?"

Owen shook his head. "I've not been here that long. I haven't got enough to take."

Quade stared across the yard at Tilton and the boy. "Your boy?"

"No." Again Owen didn't elaborate.

"Takin' him along?"

"Have to."

"Looks like a real good boy. Quiet. Steady, like a man."

"Never had much chance to be a boy. Never had any other boys to play with. All he's had is me."

"Think a lot of him, don't you?"

Scobey stared at him steadily. "I do." Yes. He thought a lot of Matt. Seeing the boy with Tilton made him feel uneasy again.

Yesterday morning, he'd thought he was safe, that he'd hidden himself successfully. Now Tilton, who knew his secret, was here. He was committed to several months' association with the man, during which time any number of things could develop. He was committed to drive Kate's cattle to Kansas, where, probably, he would encounter others who also knew.

Was Matt's respect and love for him great enough to withstand the kind of shock he was likely to get?

Scobey doubted it. And he felt the icy clutch of fear in his belly.

He said, "Make yourself comfortable in the barn loft, Mr. Quade. We'll start the gather tomorrow."

He got up and wandered over toward the barn. He caught the edge of Tilton's voice. ". . . so this sheriff's deputy called to him to drop his gun. Man turned, he did, shovin' his arms out away from his body. Deputy shot. Claimed later he thought the man was goin' for his gun. Only, I was there. I saw it. You see, boy, just because a man wears a star don't mean he's always right. This one was a dirty murderer and wherever he is right now, he knows that's what he was."

Fury blazed in Owen. He felt his fists clench tight.

He called, "Matt!"

Matt looked around. He got up at once and came to Owen. "What's the matter, Mr. Scobey?"

Owen fought himself. "Nothing. Nothing, I guess." He forced a grin. "What kind of tall tales has he been telling you?"

Matt said uneasily, "Something's the matter, Mr. Scobey. I can tell. You and me's been partners too long for—"

"We'll stay partners, too, young Matt." He was suddenly remembering Matt at seven, a solemn little boy, terrified and lonely. He remembered the way Matt had cried at night when he thought Owen was asleep. He remembered, too, that daytimes, Matt never shed a tear or complained. The boy's bravery had deepened his own feeling of remorse and guilt so much that he's spent his nights sleeplessly reviewing every small action of that fateful day, trying to assure himself that he had made no mistake.

And he could still remember every small detail of the scene, so often had he gone over it in his mind.

He said, "Think you're going to like this cattle drive? It'll be mighty hard work, but maybe you won't be as lonesome as you've been."

"I ain't been lonesome with you, Mr. Scobey."

"Haven't."

The boy said dutifully, "Haven't. Yes, sir. I haven't been lonesome with you. But going to Kansas—I'll like going to Kansas, Mr. Scobey."

"Then we'll go." Owen put his hand on the boy's shoulder. It was small, but it was hard with muscle. His throat suddenly felt tight and he turned abruptly away. Matt stood looking after him, puzzlement in his eyes. Then he turned and trotted back to where the gunman was.

Owen strode angrily toward the house. Tilton was trying to scare him now. Relating that story to the boy, omitting only names. He'd get Matt thoroughly familiar with the yarn. He'd make Matt sympathetic with the man the deputy had killed, contemptuous of the deputy himself. Then if it developed that he couldn't make Owen stay in line, he'd tell the boy who the deputy had been, who the dead man had been. That would be all it would take.

It would take a month to gather a herd of Pryor's cattle; another two, at least, to make the drive. They'd all be together for three long months.

Tilton had a club. But if he used it, Owen would kill him. He promised himself that.

He went into the house. Kate, standing at the stove, turned her head.

Most of her sunburn was gone. It hadn't blistered, but he guessed that it would peel. Oddly, she looked smaller and more womanly dressed in his oversized pants and shirt than she did in her own dress.

Her cheeks were wet with tears that she immediately and self-consciously wiped away with the back of her hand.

Like Matt, a strong, proud one who grieved in private, who presented only courageousness to the world. He said, "I'm sorry."

"Thank you. My father and I were very close. It's hard. . . ."

"Yes." He knew that it was hard. His wife and infant son had been burned to death in a fire while he'd been away with the Union troops. Perhaps his own loss explained why he'd changed course and brought young Matt south with him. Perhaps he'd been thinking of his own small son. . . .

A phrase occured to him, and this was strange because it had been years since he'd been in a church. "The Lord giveth and the Lord taketh away. . . ."

He crossed to one of the rifle ports and stared outside. Quade was leaving the shade of the house and heading for the barn. He was staring steadily at Tilton and as he went past the rifle port, Scobey got a clear, brief look at his face.

There was hatred in it—quiet, steady and implacable—the look seen sometimes in the face of a fanatical man of God who hates evil every hour of every day.

Owen's uneasiness increased. He wished he hadn't agreed to help take Kate's cattle north. Not that he'd had much choice.

But there were too many undercurrents. There was Tilton's greed, which would not be satisfied with a ten-per-cent cut if he thought he could get any more. There was this unexpectedly revealed hate in

Quade for Tilton. And there was Chavez, silent almost to the point of surliness, uncommunicative, brooding. . . .

There was also himself—hiding a guilty secret and willing to do almost anything to keep it hidden.

His eye caught dust rising distinctly out on the plain and he focused his eyes on it. A figure approaching, walking along through the knee-high grass.

Owen left the rifle port and went outside. He squinted against the glare.

The figure drew closer and he could see that it was a man wearing the blue, dusty uniform of the Cavalry.

Quade joined him and so did Tilton and Matt. Chavez slipped up behind them, a silent shadow, his swarthy face devoid of expression.

The man came down the slope and walked directly to them. He was tall, young, dark of hair and eye. His teeth flashed white as he grinned at them. He said, "Gentlemen. I understand you're driving cattle north."

Quade said dryly, "And you decided to join us."

The man grinned cheerfully again. "Right." He looked at Owen, then stuck out his hand. "Lincoln Smith, sir. My friends all call me Linc."

Owen took his hand. "Deserter?"

"Let's just say I resigned in favor of employment that promises to pay me better."

"I haven't said I'd take you on."

The man grinned impudently. "But you will. Because you need more men."

Owen said, "A deserter is a damn poor risk. If he'll desert one place, he'll desert another."

"But not until after he's been paid. And after that, who cares?"

Tilton said flatly, "You need him, Scobey."

Owen scowled. He did need Smith. He needed all the help he could get. Kate wanted to take a thousand cattle north and driving that many required men. He nodded. "All right. Five per cent is what you get. But I'll not hide you from the troopers if they come looking for you. And I'll not refuse to give you up."

Smith shrugged. His grin didn't waver, "Fair enough. Mr. Scobey. Fair enough. When do we start?"

"Tomorrow. At daybreak. Find yourself a place to sleep in the loft of the barn. And no smoking up there."

The little group dispersed. Kate came from the door of the house and stood staring curiously at the new arrival, shading her eyes with a hand. He saw her, changed course and headed toward her. Owen strode across to cut him off, but could not do so without hurrying noticeably.

He arrived as the soldier swept off his dusty hat before Kate. "Ma'am. Your servant."

A mocking light in the young soldier's eyes made a stain rise into Kate's cheeks. Owen said grouchily, "Miss Pryor, this is Lincoln Smith. He's a deserter, but he wants to help us make the drive. I hired him."

The eyes of the pair clung and Kate's sparkled suddenly with anger. Owen felt a rising irritability. He said shortly, "Your quarters are in the barn, Mr. Smith."

The man grinned at him, switched his grin to Kate, then turned and strode away. Owen said cruelly, "You're blushing like a schoolgirl."

Her eyes flashed with volatile fury. Her hand swung and collided sharply with the side of his face, stinging, burning, raising his anger instantly. He caught her by the arms, just above her elbows. He said, "Let's get one thing straight—" And then he stopped. He was acting like a schoolboy himself. A jealous schoolboy. Besides, he was as angry with Lincoln Smith for his brash impudence as he was with Kate.

He said, "Never mind."

He released her and watched her run angrily toward the house. The scowl on his face deepened as his uneasy feeling of premonition grew. Now they had a ladies' man to add to an already tangled and motley crew.

He stared across the yard at the men grouped before the barn. Not a one of them but what was dangerous in his way. Each had his own private drives, each a different reason for going along.

Tilton would try for more than ten per cent, using his knowledge of Owen's past as a kind of vicious pry. Quade, for reasons unknown, hated Tilton savagely. Lincoln Smith was an engaging opportunist, without principals. He'd be after Kate like a dog after a bitch in heat. Chavez was an enigma, but Owen felt instinctively that he was perhaps the most dangerous of the lot.

He turned away, still scowling. His judgements had been harsh. But better harsh than too soft now. Better to be on guard.

☆ 6 ☆

THEY rode out in the first gray light of dawn, heading east toward the vast, unfenced range occupied by the thousands of longhorned beasts that wore the Spanish Spur.

Owen's wagon went along, carrying supplies, blankets, food, and driven by Quade, who had volunteered for the job. Kate rode the wagon with him. Matt, mounted, rode along behind.

Owen had been immeasurably relieved when Quade volunteered for the wagon job. To him it meant that Kate was safe, that Matt was safe. He felt he could trust Quade. More, at least, than any of the others.

Kate had expressed a desire to see her house once more, and so they went directly there, intending to make it their temporary base of operations. The wagon wrote straight twin tracks upon the ground and the men, with Owen in charge, combed a strip of country five miles wide as they rode along behind.

For a country that looked as flat as this, there were many places in which cattle shaded up during the worst heat of the day. In ravines choked with brush. In boulder fields where a man could see no

46

farther than three hundred yards in any direction. In hollows hidden from him until he rode down their shallow rims.

But the herd grew steadily as men rode in from right and left, bringing small bunches they had gathered along the way.

Steers, mostly. But old range bulls, too. And dry heifers and cows wherever they were found.

Lincoln Smith rode alone on the far right, next to him Tilton, next to him Owen Scobey himself. On Scobey's left rode Jesus Chavez, silent, taciturn, almost sullen. But Chavez brought in his share of steers.

At noon, Scobey consented to let young Matt drive the herd. And after that, he was never far from its rising dust in case the boy should need his help.

Their number was not enough; his trust in them was not enough. They were a sorry crew but they were all he had. Certainly they were tough enough; he need not worry about the safety of any of them.

And at sundown, he could not complain about the amount of work that has been done. Even after cutting the old animals, out, he was left with eighty-seven head, certainly a good start for the opening day.

Kate's house was blackened on its inside walls, around its rifle ports and its burned-out door. Its roof, beneath which brush and beams had been consumed, had fallen in, effectively burying anything that might be left. But she went inside and dug in the ruins until her hands and face and clothes were black.

The others left her alone. After a time, she came backing out, dragging a metal trunk behind. She rummaged inside the trunk in the semidarkness of approaching night, got some clothes from it and disappeared in the direction of the dry stream bed. There was a hole there like the one Owen had dug in his own stream bed, a hole in which she probably intended to bathe.

Owen sat silent and watchful beside the fire. Lincoln Smith stirred and rose. Owen said coldly, "Stay put."

Smith grinned at him, but there was a certain unpleasant light behind his eyes. He settled back, but his eyes continued to rest on Owen's face. "Just going to ask her if I could wear some of her father's clothes," he said.

"Wear the ones you've got on."

"Not in Kansas. You think I want to be shot?"

Owen repeated implacably, "Wear the ones you've got on."

"Maybe before I'm through, I'll be wearing yours." There was a nasty edge to Smith's voice.

Owen got to his feet. He knew what he was going to do. Maybe he could let this small incident blow past, but sooner or later, he was going to have to make it very plain to Lincoln Smith and to the others as well that they remained united or died. He said softly, "Try taking them now, Mr. Smith."

"I didn't mean—"

"Oh, yes you did, Mr. Smith. You meant exactly what you said. Now back it up or everyone here is going to think you're as yellow as I think you are."

Smith snatched for his gun in the Cavalry holster at his side. Owen didn't even bother to draw his own. Instead, he kicked with deadly accuracy.

Smith never even got the holster unsnapped. He howled as Scobey's boot struck his wrist, and leaped instinctively away.

Owen was cold and precise as he moved on in.

He knew he wasn't enforcing discipline—not altogether. He knew he wasn't administering punishment for an infraction. Nor was he protecting Kate.

He was seeking an outlet for his own uneasiness and knew it, and didn't care. The end of enforcing discipline would be served by his action. Kate would be safer because of it. A worse blowup might be prevented later on.

He liked the solid feel of Smith's jaw beneath his bony fist. He liked the way the man's eyes glazed briefly as he staggered back. He liked the wicked light of battle that came into Smith's reckless eyes.

It told him something he'd wanted to know. For all his unscrupulousness, Smith was not a coward.

Owen even liked the pain of Smith's fist landing on the side of his neck. Because it dissipated any doubts that might have remained in him.

He bored in mercilessly, chopping with short rights and lefts, bruising, cutting. Smith backed away, covering, occasionally striking back. Owen absorbed the blows as though they were nothing at all.

Five years of hiding, of fearing, of doubting himself. Five years while it all boiled around in his mind. Five years of helpless inactivity. Now he released it all and Lincoln Smith was overwhelmed.

The man went down, cursing savagely. He got up, went down again. Then he turned and ran, dragging at the covered holster in a frantic effort to get his gun clear.

Owen pursued, dived at Smith and brought him crashing to the ground. The revolver tumbled away, to be lost in the darkness. Smith scrambled on, his eyes on a rifle lying beside the leaping fire.

The others moved out of his way, watching this

with impassive, neutral eyes. Smith reached the rifle, seized it, swung it around and brought it to bear.

The gun bellowed. Smoke that appeared white in the fire's light billowed from its muzzle.

Owen felt the sear of the bullet along the side of his thigh. Then he was on the man.

The rifle swung and the barrel clipped him solidly in the side of the head. Dizziness rose in waves. He staggered directly toward the fire.

He would fall into it. And while he was recovering, Smith would finish him off with a second shot.

His legs pumped furiously as he tried desperately to recover his balance. He failed. He fell into the leaping flames, rolled convulsively the instant he felt its coals beneath him.

The rifle roared almost in his face. The bullet scattered a shower of sparks that rose with the smoke into the still night air.

Owen continued to roll almost frantically, with a double purpose. He had to extinguish his smoldering clothing or he would become, as he fought, a living torch. And he had to avoid the bullets probing for him, bullets which came as fast as Smith could lever and fire the rifle.

He gained his feet at last. He charged directly at the man, not caring now for the rifle still firmly in the man's two hands and pointed directly at his chest.

Smith triggered just as Matt threw himself at him. The boy's body, colliding with his legs, upset his aim and the bullet tore harmlessly into the ground at Owen's feet. Then Owen was on Smith.

He seized the rifle, tore it from the man's hands and flung it aside. He snatched Smith bodily from the ground and threw him into the fire's light.

Smith staggered up, to meet Owen's savagely

chopping fist that drove him back and down. This time he lay quite still, visibly breathing but still unconscious.

Owen slapped at a smoldering spot on his thigh, burned his hand and cursed breathlessly. He stared at Matt, who stood with white face and terror-stricken eyes, watching him.

He grinned, a slow, easy grin that brought the color back into Matt's scared face. "Thanks, boy. Thanks. That one would have got me sure."

Then he turned and faced Tilton and Quade. He said coldly, "This isn't a deal where everybody's got a say in what is done. You do what I say or you fight. That clear enough?"

Quade said, "It's clear." There was the slightest of grins on his ancient face and he stood at Tilton's right and a step behind, his hand almost touching the grip of his gun.

Owen realized with a shock that Quade was hoping Hilton would take it up. If Tilton did, he'd be shot before he could touch his gun.

He supposed he should have been glad for Quade's unspoken support, but it made him uneasy instead of pleased. Before the drive was finished, Quade would kill Tilton if he could.

And Owen's crew was pitifully small at best. One man could spell the difference between success, failure or death.

He saw Kate standing at the edge of the fire's light, watching him. She startled him because she had bathed and dressed herself in woman's clothes. She had brushed her hair and tied it up behind her head.

Her eyes were inscrutable and he couldn't tell whether she approved of what he had done or disapproved. He walked toward her, touched as once before by a kind of ache inside.

He scarcely knew her and therefore couldn't love her. What ate at him was a man's eternal yearning for the things a woman could provide—gentleness, softness in a harsh, hard world of men. An easing of the primitive hungers that ever plague a lonely man.

He said, "You saw that?"

She nodded wordlessly.

He said, "It will probably happen again. I do not want you to interfere."

"I won't interfere." He couldn't understand the expression on her face and in her eyes. He couldn't have put a name to the emotion causing it if he tried. He relaxed ever so slightly and said, "You're very pretty in that dress."

"Thank you."

"But I'd rather you would wear the clothes you were wearing before."

"Why?"

Impatience stirred him. "Lincoln Smith already has his eyes on you. So has Tilton. These are lonely men and I'll have my hands full controlling them as it is. No sense making it any worse."

She flushed deeply, and her eyes avoided his. He said, "Besides that, we'll be watched and trailed by Indians a good part of the way. If they don't know a woman is with us, they'll be much more likely to keep away."

She said shortly, "I'll change."

"And bathing—cut it to a minimum. When you have to bathe, let me know and I'll stand guard."

She glanced up and for the first time, there was mocking amusement on her face. "Are you the only one with whom I'm safe, Mr. Scobey? Are you the only one not made with feet of clay?"

It was Owen's turn for discomfort. He said coldly, "You want your cattle driven north. I'll try and do that part of the job. Beyond that—"

"Beyond that, you take your life the way it is, don't you Mr. Scobey? You don't want women complicating things. Don't worry. I'll not complicate your life. I want no part of you."

She was angry now, but maybe it was better so. Owen grinned at her. "All men don't turn to jelly when a woman looks at them."

Her face turned white. She bit her lip savagely. She said softly, fiercely, "Damn you!" turned and ran into the darkness toward the house.

Irritability caused the basic uneasiness in Owen Scobey to grow. This would be one hell of an undertaking, because already everybody was at everybody else's throat.

☆ 7 ☆

OWEN SCOBEY turned and headed for the fire. Around him, the night was black and still. Those at the fire watched him steadily, with varying expressions in their eyes.

Matt's expression was one of puzzlement touched with unease. Scobey reached over, gripped the boy's shoulder briefly and smiled. Matt had never seen him in a fight. He had never seen him completely and furiously angry. The smile and the touch seemed to reassure the boy.

Tilton's glance was a warning, and to make it plainer, he said distinctly, "Don't ever try to use me like that, Scobey, or I'll kill you where you stand. Besides spillin' your bag of beans."

"Then don't behave like that."

Quade was ancient, watchful and taciturn. As always, his hand was never far from his gun, his eyes never away from Tilton for long. He reminded Owen of a caged and hungry beast staring at live prey through the bars of his cage. His hunger would continue, but if he watched and waited and was patient, the bars of the cage might melt away.

Lincoln Smith stirred, opened his eyes and

struggled up to a sitting position. Owen stared coldly at him. "Get up and relieve Chavez with the herd."

Rebellion flared in Smith's eyes, then died away. He got up and shuffled sullenly to his horse. Owen heard the fast, staccato beat of the animal's hoofs diminishing and dying out.

Again the night was still. Tilton headed for his blanket roll at the edge of the firelight. Quade stiffly followed suit. Owen said softly, "Better go on to bed, Matt. Morning gets here mighty soon."

There was still puzzlement in Matt's young eyes, but his uneasiness was gone. He did not—could not—understand why Owen had reacted so violently to Smith's seemingly harmless desire to leave the fire. He was still too young to know the savagery that drives some men where women are concerned.

Even now, Owen wasn't sure that fear of consequences would restrain Smith. He had not liked the look that had been in Smith's eyes as Kate disappeared toward the stream. They had mirrored the thoughts going on in his mind, flaring and turning hot as he thought of Kate disrobing there to bathe.

Best thing to do would be to cut Smith loose and send him south, but he couldn't spare the man. He didn't know how thoroughly Captain Richards could cleanse the country to northward of the hostile bands. He needed a man on point, Chavez probably, to scout the land ahead and lay a course. He needed two flankers, himself and Tilton. He needed a man with the horses and would use Smith for this. Quade could drive the wagon.

Kate could cook and young Matt could ride the drag. There just weren't any spares. And if they had to fight, there wouldn't be enough.

Matt crawled into his blankets and lay starring at the leaping flames. Scobey replenished the fire, then walked away into the night. He saw Chavez ride in from the direction of the herd. He walked on, frowning to himself.

Funny, the things that determine the course of a man's life. Conger's boy, orphaned, had had perhaps the most profound effect on his. But now there was this—Kate, Tilton, the drive itself.

Nothing remained static, he guessed. He had been a fool to think it could.

He heard something on the slope of a hill and stopped to listen closely. The fire, the shapes of the men sleeping beside it, were small and indistinct with distance.

The sound was a woman's voice, Kate's voice, praying at the grave of her parents.

Reciting the prayers she had learned as a child. "The Lord is my shepard, I shall not want. He maketh me to lie down in green pastures. He leadeth me beside . . ."

A young voice, soft, uncertain, and yet somehow filled with strength, with faith. He could use a little of her faith, he thought. His own, right now, was small and weak.

He let himself think briefly of what might happen to her if anything happened to him. Smith, for all his slyness and greed, would be unable to restrain himself. He'd use her and when his lust was spent, would throw her aside. . . .

Tilton would use her in a different way in a coldly calculating way. He would want from her a different thing—her land, her cattle. . . .

Chavez would probably have no interest in her and if it was up to him, would abandon her someplace on the trackless plain to find her own way to safety if she could. Quade might try and see her to safety if doing so did not restrict his chance to avenge himself on Tilton.

And Matt . . . Not one of them save Quade, perhaps, would care for Matt.

For Kate's safety, for Matt's, he ought to give up this drive. He ought to refuse to go, and let Tilton tell the boy the truth. He'd had five years in which to win the boy's affection and trust. A few words weren't going to destroy all that.

But he knew he lied to himself. The words Tilton could utter would destroy all that.

So immersed was he in his own gloomy thoughts that he started as Kate came walking softly down the slope. She saw him, called in a hesitant, frightened voice, "Is that you, Mr. Scobey?"

He said, "Yes."

She said simply, "They were all I had and I loved them very much."

He didn't reply, not knowing what to say to her.

She said, "Matt—he loves you that way, Mr. Scobey. You must have been very good to him."

"I've tried. I don't know—"

She said, "There is something you have to hide from Matt, isn't there?"

"Yes." The word slipped out.

"And Mr. Tilton knows what it is?"

"Yes."

"And that is why you are going on this drive?"

"That's why."

"Don't you think we can make it?"

He was silent for several moments, saying at last, "I think we have a chance of making it, but not a very good chance. We are too few. We have no one we can trust except ourselves. Quade hates Tilton. I don't know why. But he hates him enough to want to kill him."

"Then why doesn't he do it? Why hasn't he done it before?"

Owen shrugged. He didn't know the answer to that himself. He decided suddenly that Quade wanted more than Tilton's death. He wanted the man broken, ruined, on the brink of despair. Then and only then could he satisfy the hatred that festered in his mind.

He said, "Tilton isn't going to be satisfied with his ten per cent."

"I suspected that."

"And you're willing to risk it?"

Her voice was patient. "Mr. Scobey, I have no choice. I must risk anything or leave this land. And I will not leave."

Patient, but touched with steel. Her face was a blur to him in the blackness of the night.

He said, "Lincoln Smith is the most dangerous of all to you. Be careful with him. Don't let yourself be caught alone. . . ."

She said softly, "Then that fight—with Smith—was because of me?"

"He wanted to follow you to the stream."

She was silent and he knew he had frightened her. Good. She needed some fright in her to make her cautious.

He said, "Sleep close to the fire."

"All right, Mr. Scobey." She moved away, for the first time a frightened, helpless girl dependent on a man's protection. The fear of death had left her untouched. She had faced it and beaten it. But this was something else. Raised out here with her parents and the few Mexican *vaqueros* her father occasionally hired her only human contacts, she was as sheltered and protected as a girl can be. This was her first inkling that love had many twisted faces.

Scobey watched her silhouetted against the fire's light as she approached it. He watched her settle down her blankets close to Matt's small and sleeping form.

He frowned, knew he should turn in, and yet did not. He stared at the sleeping forms around the fire.

Mostly he had them pegged and knew that he must watch each for Chavez, however, remained an enigma.

Why had the tracker consented to make the drive? Owen felt sure money didn't interest him. He was too much animal, too much a man of the wilderness for that.

Not a man that mixed with other men. Not one with much interest in women, either.

But a man to watch, thought Owen.

Uneasiness touched his mind again, uneasiness that almost amounted to premonition. The drive would not succeed. Death and destruction would follow it to Kansas. The lives of each of those who went along would be threatened and would change.

Yet he knew he would not back out. He was committed to make the drive, even forced to make it, whether he wanted to or not.

He could only be watchful and ready for whatever might turn up. He could only wait, and hope.

☆ 8 ☆

THEY were up with the dawn, taciturn and silent men, each taking care of his own needs, putting away his bedroll, catching and saddling his horse, wandering off toward the hole in the stream bed to wash.

Owen built a fire and Kate prepared breakfast from the stores carried in the wagon. The men hunkered around the fire, eating silently from tin plates, drinking bitter coffee made from beans. Only Matt seemed to be looking forward to the day.

Owen ordered Quade to stay with the cattle gathered yesterday. He caught and saddled a horse for Kate and told her to stay close to Quade after she got the camp cleaned up.

She had dressed this morning, obediently, in the clothes Owen had given her instead of in the dress she'd worn last night. Her eyes were a bit frightened as she watched him ride away with Matt, as though worried about this thing she had set in motion, this drive.

Quade watched Tilton steadily as the man rode past the gathered herd and Tilton, aware of the scrutiny, stared straight ahead, frowning slightly. Not afraid, thought Owen. Puzzled. Sensing now for the first time that Quade felt some personal animosity toward him.

Chavez, following Tilton, seemed unaware of either Tilton or Quade. He rode with his eyes on the ground, reading it the way civilized men read the pages of a book. Occasionally, his head would rise and though not noticeably doing so, he would sweep the surrounding area with his eyes.

Smith followed Chavez, his head turned for a last look at Kate, who was already at work cleaning up the camp. He felt Owen's scowling scrutiny and glanced at him. There was a sudden, smoldering challenge in his reckless eyes, something that said as plainly as any words could say, "You stopped me once, but you won't always be around."

Beyond the loosely bunched cattle, Tilton halted his horse and turned. Chavez and Smith caught up in turn and halted, too. They watched Owen approach without enthusiasm.

Owen halted his horse, with Matt close beside him. The sky in the east was turning pink as the sun crept toward the horizon's rim. Owen said, "We'll work to the north of here first." He pointed toward a shadowy line of low hills covered with the grayish streaks that indicated brushy cover. Nearer, dark patches on the plains were clumps of thick mesquite. He said, "Spread out. Tilton on the right, Smith next. Matt will push along the ones we gather and I'll ride Matt's left. Chavez on the far left. Work out all those clumps of mesquite even though it is a bit early for anything to be shaded up in them."

Tilton's eyes rested challengingly on Owen's face. "I was goin' to ask the boy to ride with me."

Matt's face brightened. He looked at Owen. "Can I, Owen?" Owen could not fail to notice Matt's use of his first name, but he was not displeased. It seemed to bring Matt closer.

Tilton grinned. "He likes a good yarn, that boy. And Beecher Tilton is sure the man that can spin one."

Owen said sourly, "No time for yarns. You ride alone."

Matt's face settled into a pattern of resentment. Tilton grinned mockingly both at Owen's scowl and at Matt's disappointment. He said, "We'll spin our yarns in camp, boy." He turned and rode away at a rocking lope.

The others took their positions and the line moved north. Most times, Owen could see neither Matt on his right nor Chavez on his left.

It was a long time before his scowl faded. Tilton was already beginning to undermine the closeness between him and Matt. He was doing it slowly and skillfully now, knowing that Matt's resentment must be gradually roused. But it would continue and Tilton's criticism of Owen would become more edged and sharp with the passage of time.

Tilton wanted to ingratiate himself with the boy, make Matt like and respect him. Thus he would increase the hold he had over Owen for whatever dark use he intended to put that hold to later on. Matt's loyalty at this moment was wholly with Owen. While Owen couldn't chance it, he knew that Tilton's accusation that Owen had killed Matt's father might now conceivably be met with skepticism or even outright disbelief. Later, though, after Tilton had won the boy's trust, it would be a different story. Particularly if Matt's resentment had been raised deliberately and skillfully before Tilton told him how his father had died.

Owen scowled again as he entered a thicket of

mesquite. It was a small thicket but it yielded two heifers and a steer. He pushed them out beyond and headed them northeast.

Even at this point, there could be little doubt as to what purpose Tilton meant to use his hold, he thought. There could be but one reason for building it up this way. He would not be satisfied with his ten-per-cent cut of the herd when they had reached Kansas with it. He would want it all.

When that time came, Owen would— His jaw hardened. He was forewarned. He believed he knew Tilton's intentions. So he would use the man as Tilton was using him, to get the herd to Kansas. After that had been done, he would find a way to cope with Tilton and his threats. He'd kill him if he must.

The morning passed slowly, still and hot. By mid-morning, he was no longer finding cattle in the open. He found them now only in the thickets, where there was shade, where there was thorny branches to scrape away the flies.

Chavez brought him a bunch of fourteen and he added the dozen he had gathered to them and took them eastward. Matt was already driving more than twenty head. Owen let his bunch join them, then dropped back and grinned cheerfully at the boy.

Matt's eyes were puzzled and broody and that was unusual for him. He said, "You don't like Mr. Tilton, do you?"

"No."

"Why? You don't even know him."

Owen said, "I know his kind, boy."

"That isn't fair, Owen. I like him."

Owen stared at him closely, knowing he had already lost something to Tilton, however small it might be now. "Why do you like him?"

Matt puzzled over that a few moments in his sober, grown-up way. He looked small riding a full-sized horse. Watching him, Owen's chest felt tight. His throat seemed to close briefly.

Matt said, "I don't know, Owen. I just do. I like to listen to him talk. Seems like he's been every place and done everything."

Owen opened his mouth to speak, then snapped it shut. Telling Matt that Tilton was a cold-blooded killer wouldn't do a bit of good. Not without proof. Not without details. And maybe it wouldn't help even then. Matt would have to see Tilton for what he was. He would have to see Tilton do the things Owen had indirectly accused him of before he would believe.

He said, "Don't try to keep them bunched too close. It'll make them hard to hold. Just ease 'em along north and let them graze as they go."

"All right, Owen."

Owen rode away again. Almost out of sight, he looked back. He saw a horseman approaching the boy, driving a small bunch ahead of him.

Tilton. But there was no use worrying about one day. Tilton had weeks to snare the boy's friendship and loyalty.

He worked on, scowling and silent and with angry, brooding eyes. At sundown, they returned to camp, driving ahead of them the gather for the day.

Each succeeding day was like the last and they blended together with weary monotony. Pressure was on them all, pressure they felt and could not escape. Richards had driven the Comanches north, but Richards had been nearly out of supplies when he passed through here. His men were tired. He would take his command south again and when he did, the Comanches would return.

So they worked—from dawn to dusk—and took turns at night herding the cattle and slept fewer hours because they did.

No longer did the men walk to the stream to wash and shave when morning came. Now they got out of their bedrolls tousled, dirty and red-eyed. And remained that way all day.

Tempers grew touchy. Tilton found it hard to be civil to Matt, though he tried desperately and obviously to continue the campaign he had begun. He glowered at Quade every time he passed him in camp or on the plain. And Quade glowered back with smoldering, openly hating eyes.

Chavez, though plainly taking the grueling days better than any of the others, showed weariness, too. Its effect on him was to make him even more silent and taciturn than before. Occasionally, Owen spoke to him, telling him to take a night-herding watch or do something else connected with the roundup itself, but he never replied more than a noncommittal grunt or nod.

And Smith—the everlasting weariness even seemed to have taken some of the heat out of his desire for Kate, though he watched her ceaselessly the way a cat may watch a bird. He watched her and Kate grew uneasy and afraid.

But the herd grew, too. At the end of the first week, they had close to five hundred head. The second week brought fewer, but at the end of the third, they were almost done, having gathered a herd of nearly a thousand head.

Gradually, as the herd grew in size, it took more and more out of the men to loose-herd it during the day. Kate and Quade and Matt and Chavez were with them now all day, riding the perimeter of the herd, moving stragglers back. Smith stayed with the horse herd. Which left only Owen and Tilton to continue the gather and necessarily slowed it down.

They rode out each morning and returned each night. They began to bring in the older steers, the longhorned ones, the ones who were wily and smart enough to have escaped the earlier search for them.

Owen lived in his saddle these days. He slept at night with the reins of the horse tied to his wrist. Each time he came in, he roped and saddled a fresh horse to replace the one he had completely worn out in a few short hours of riding. And Tilton did the same.

What few encounters they had with each other were snarling, snappish ones. Owen began to hope Tilton's self-control would break. He began to hope for a showdown, which could only end with one of them dead on the ground.

But it didn't come. Nothing happened until the last day of the roundup, the day he decided they had enough.

At sundown, they were still several miles from camp. Ahead of them they drove six longhorned steers and two young dry cows. There was one in the bunch, one steer whose horns were thick and long and curved. A steer with red, rolling eyes, with a solid blue-roan coat of half-shed winter hair. A bunch-quitter.

Owen would probably have to let him go, aware that the animal would give them trouble all the way to the Kansas line. But Tilton, short-tempered and edgy anyway, thought differently. To Tilton, the steer was an outlet for his irritable rage.

Three times he returned the steer to the bunch. The fourth time the animal quit the bunch and hightailed it for a nearby mesquite clump, Tilton spurred widly after him, shaking out his loop.

It was an old trick, but one that nearly always worked. If you roped and dumped a bunch-quitter every time he quit the bunch, if you spilled him hard enough to drive the breath from him, he soon gave up trying to quit the bunch. Only this wasn't a steer you could count on dumping every time. Six or seven years old, he must have weighed fifteen hundred pounds. His back was as tall as the back of a horse, and he was wild and mean.

Tilton's loop hissed out, settled neatly over the steer's great horns. Tilton hauled his mount to a hasty halt.

The steer hit the end of the rope and it twanged taut like a fiddlestring being tuned. The steer's neck bent sharply and he struck the ground.

Tilton's saddle and Tilton himself hit the ground at almost the same instant. Tilton's horse bolted.

Owen Scobey started to grin. He was almost a quarter mile away and could not see Tilton's face. But he could imagine the expression it wore. His grin widened in spite of himself.

Tilton and the steer fought to their feet at almost the same moment and stood glaring at each other. Tilon's hand shot to his side.

But no gun came up; no shot cracked out. Tilton turned his head to search the ground for his gun.

The steer pawed the ground, lowered his head and shook it back and forth. Owen sank his spurs into his own mount's sides.

It had been funny a moment ago—Tilton afoot and so mad his rage was visible at a quarter mile. It wasn't funny any more. In seconds, that steer was going to charge, either to impale Tilton on the knife-sharp points of his horns or trample him into the ground.

Owen raked the sides of his horse frantically with the spurs. The animal ran.

In this instant, Owen didn't remember he hated Tilton and feared the knowledge Tilton had threatened to use. He didn't even think that holding back would be a sure and easy way of ridding himself of the lanky gunfighter.

He shook out his own rope as the distance narrowed to two hundred yards—to a hundred. The steer didn't see him but Tilton did. He stood like a bullfighter, poised to leap right or left as the steer charged.

While Owen was still nearly a hundred yards away, the steer lumbered into motion, relatively slow at first but increasing speed the way a train does with the distance it travels down the track.

Owen swerved slightly to intercept the steer. His rope sang out. . . .

It settled over the steer's horns. Owen, as Tilton had, hauled his horse to a halt and braced himself for the shock.

The steer hit the end of the rope only a dozen feet from the man he was trying to kill. Owen's saddle shifted. His horse jerked and almost lost his footing. But the steer went down and Owen's saddle cinch held.

Tilton scrambled out of the tumbling steer's way. Owen rode to the animal, lying stunned from the fall. He shook his rope, thus loosening the loop resting over the animal's horns. He flipped it clear. He stepped off his horse, flipped Tilton's rope off, then remounted. The steer wheezed mightily, several times and struggled groggily to his feet. He glared at Owen and at Tilton beyond him. Then he turned and trotted back in the direction of the bunch.

With the urgency of the action gone, Owen could

think of the opportunity he had allowed to pass him by. He said sourly, "I should have let the bastard put a horn through you."

Tilton scowled at him. "Don't think I owe you anything because you didn't. I'd have made out all right."

Owen stared down at him for several moments. Tilton met his stare mockingly. Then he turned and began to search the ground for his gun.

Owen coiled his rope and rode after Tilton's horse. He roped him and led him back.

Tilton was splicing the cinch with leather lacing. Owen took his loop off Tilton's horse. He rode away without speaking, leaving Tilton to saddle up and follow when he could.

He was sorry now, and bitterly cursing himself for his foolishness. He regretted saving Tilton and knew he would regret it more before he reached Kansas with the herd. The action had been instinctive rather than thoughtful.

But what was done was done. There was no alternative now but to make the best of it.

☆ 9 ☆

Owen slept as though he were dead until he was called at midnight for his night-herding shift. He pulled on his boots, crammed his hat on his head and swung to the saddle of his horse, only now untying the reins from his wrist.

He rode out in the cool night and took the place of Quade, who had wakened him.

Exhaustion had increased his feeling of hopelessness and despair. Groggy and half asleep in his saddle, he circled the herd halfway until he met Chavez, then turned and rode the other way. At least, he thought, there would be no need for trail-branding the herd. They all wore the Spanish Spur. There were no other cattle for a hundred miles around.

The hours dragged, but at last the sky in the east began to show a touch of gray. Shortly thereafter, Smith rode out and relieved him to eat.

He returned to camp. The others were up. Quade and Kate were readying the wagon to start, hitching it up, tying down anything that might move, lashing water kegs in place. They all finished eating, killed the fire and saddled up.

Chavez took point, for upon him would fall the

burden of selecting the trail and finding water. Tilton rode flank on the right, Owen on the left. Matt brought up the drag, a dirty job but one he could handle and certainly the safest of the lot.

The wagon traveled slowly on the far right flank, with Quade driving. Smith moved the horse herd slowly along half a mile on the left.

As they moved, Owen's depression lifted momentarily. There was satisfaction in seeing the great, longhorned beasts stir and lumber north. Both he and Tilton rode at full speed back and forth along the flanks, yelling until they were hoarse, urging stragglers along.

Today would be the most difficult day of all. The herd must be broken to the trail. They must find their place in the drive. The ones who would lead needed time to take their place in the front.

Once they did this, they would assume approximately the same position every day. Before they reached Kansas, Owen would know most of them by sight, would know their idiosyncrasies and would even have given some of them names. He would know what to expect from each of them.

At noon, they had covered less than five miles. Owen had worn out three horses, Tilton two. But the cattle were grazing slowly north of their own free will. The worst of it was past.

Briefly Owen halted his horse on a little rise and stared down at the slowly moving herd.

They were strung out for a mile or more. Dust rose in a cloud, not the dust of swift movement but that of slow-moving hoofs. Occasionally, a pillar of thicker dust would rise someplace as a couple of them pawed the ground and glared at each other, or scuffled briefly.

Beyond the herd, he could see the wagon trav-

eling slowly along, necessarily taking a winding
course to avoid arroyos, brush clumps and rocky
ground. Sometimes it disappeared from sight but it
always reappeared farther on.

Owen swung his head. He hated to trust the horse
herd to Smith, who had demonstrated his untrust-
worthiness by deserting the Army. Without the
horse herd, they would be lost. Yet he had no
choice. Smith had no experience with cattle and he
did know horses. Besides that, Owen wanted him as
far as possible from the wagon and Kate.

He touched his horse's sides and rode on. The
miles passed and the hours passed, and at sundown
they halted, having traveled twelve or thirteen miles
from where they started at dawn.

Like this, the days passed, blending with monoto-
nous regularity, one into the next. The miles fell behind as steadily, a dozen a day. The herd settled
down into its unvarying routine.

The men worked, and slept, and snarled at each
other like wild animals quarreling over food. Of
them all, Chavez seemed to be the most tireless.

He rode point throughout each day. He stood his
night-herding watches along with the others. He ate
when he could, and sometimes slept. Yet he found
time for scouting, too, more time than he found for
sleep.

Owen would watch him ride off into the darkness
after relieving him on the rim of the bedded herd.
He would watch him ride away from camp instead
of toward it.

How a man could scout trail in the darkness
he didn't know. Yet when he questioned Chavez, the
man's only explanation was the spare, "Scout. Find
trail for tomorrow."

Traveling northward, Owen began to find signs

that the Comanches had returned. A trail of horsemen, never more than two or three in a group. A camp, with the ashes of a fire a blackened spot on the dusty ground. And on the ninth day out, drawn by circling vultures, he found something else, something he stopped beside while he stared down in startled horror.

It was a man—it had once been a man. Naked and horribly mutilated, it lay there on the plain, a man no more, while buzzards who had risen from it circled in impatient ugliness fifty feet in the air.

With a sinking feeling, Owen realized how this would look to any wandering Comanches who might be attracted by the buzzards after the herd had passed. The trail of the herd was less than a mile away. The tracks of Owen's horse were plain here on the ground. They would think, and with justification, that the trail drivers had tortured and killed the brave.

Owen turned away. He lifted his horse to a steady gallop and headed for the wagon. Reaching it, he said, "Quade, get on your horse. Bring a shovel."

Quade pulled the wagon to a halt. He rummaged in the back for a shovel. When he found it, he untied his saddle horse from the rear of the wagon and mounted.

Kate stared at Owen. "Is something the matter?"

"Dead Indian. I don't want to leave him unburied this close to our trail."

He looked down at her hungrily. Her face was thinner than it had been a month ago. She had lost some weight.

If anything, it made her more attractive than before, he thought. It made her eyes seem larger, her mouth softer. It made her seem smaller and more dependent. His glance held until color rose in her face and he felt, once more the the vague stirring of hunger, an ache somewhere in his chest, a need to touch her and hold her in his arms, coupled with growing worry for her safety. If anything happened to him . . .

He said, "You can drive for a while?"

"Yes."

"We'll be back soon."

He led the way around the herd. Passing the rear of it, he saw Matt plodding along in its dust. He rode to the boy.

Matt's eyes were red and rimmed with mud formed by dust and the tears it caused to flow from his eyes. He, too, had lost weight. He looked tiny and exhausted atop the horse he rode. He looked at Owen without interest.

Owen forced himself to grin. "Doing all right?"

The boy nodded wordlessly.

Owen said, "Move up on the flank awhile. Get out of the dust."

Matt nodded, turned his horse slightly and headed along the flank. Owen led on past.

The vultures had settled again and they rose a second time from the mutilated corpse, flapping thunderously, making ugly, croaking cries.

Owen swung to the ground and Quade followed suit. He stood staring down at the corpse for several moments. Owen asked, "Got any ideas?"

Quade shook his head. "Could've been a hunting party from another tribe, one that's enemies of the Comanches. Don't seem likely, though. Ain't likely they'd do this to him, either. They'd kill him and lift his hair. They'd take his horse and his gun if he had one. But I doubt they'd torture him."

Owen's eyes turned involuntarily toward the north, toward Chavez, riding point. Chavez had been scouting last night. He had come this way. . . .

He shrugged. Quade had already begun to dig. Owen watched him awhile, then took the shovel from him and finished the grave. He helped Quade lift the body and drop it in, grimacing with distaste as he did. He searched the ground for the Indian's clothing and weapons, dropped them in, then let Quade fill it in and watched as he worked at smoothing it out. When the man had finished, he said, "Now help me cut out a bunch from the herd."

Quade mounted. They rode together to the drag of the herd. Skillfully they cut out about twenty or thirty head and turned them west.

They drove the cattle directly over the grave, fighting them, forcing them when the smell of the place struck terror into them and made them want to turn aside.

Owen slipped his revolver from its holster. As the cattle passed over the grave, he selected one of the thinner, weaker ones and fired. The steer fell and did not move again.

Owen helped Quade return the cattle to the herd. Then he stopped his horse and fumbled in his pocket for tobacco.

He stared at Quade. "Think it was Chavez?"

Quade shrugged. "Could have been. He's got an outsize hate for 'em. Guess I can't blame him much. His ma hated 'em and hated him because he was one of 'em. He ran away from home when he was nine."

"He tell you this?" Owen's tone was surprised.

"Hell, no. He never told nobody nothin'. Oldster that knew him told me, down in Sonora eight, ten years back."

"You've known him a long time, then?"

"Un huh."

"You've known him to kill Comanches like this before?"

Quade grunted noncommittally. "I reckon he's kilt Injuns. I reckon he's took scalps."

"You know more about him than that."

Quade didn't reply.

"You realize that he's risking every one of our necks, don't you? He'll pull the Comanches down on us before he's through. We covered that one up. But what about the ones we don't find and can't cover up?"

"Maybe one of 'em will git him."

Owen stared at Quade a moment more. The man had as much as told him Chavez was the Indian's killer. He'd also let Owen know it was no use to interfere.

Owen watched him ride in the direction of the wagon. He gathered some stragglers and forced them along until they caught up with the remainder of the herd. He looked back at the place where they'd buried the Indian and where he'd shot the steer.

The buzzards were circling. Some of them had already alighted and were tearing at the steer.

The dead steer would explain the presence of the birds in case any Indians investigated. The cattle they'd driven over the grave would probably hide it. But his worry did not fade.

He rode on, caught up with Matt and talked to him awhile. He felt sorry for the boy's weariness. He noted with concern the way Matt had thinned down in the last few weeks.

He had no right to work young Matt this way. He should have told Tilton to go to hell and refused to make the drive. He was going to lose Matt before this was over with, anyway. He had a premonition suddenly and it turned his belly cold.

He rode on ahead, knowing he would jump Chavez about the tortured Indian brave, knowing also that Chavez, in his tight-lipped, uncommunicative way, would only deny it.

He rode up the flank of the herd, moving stragglers back. Eventually, he reached the point and rode over beside Chavez.

The man looked at him sourly, giving him the sparest of nods. He was a squat man, with heavy and slightly bowed legs. Put him in breechclout, let his hair grow and put a feather in it and he'd be indistinguishable from a Comanche, thought Owen. His Mexican ancestry didn't show at all.

He said, "Found a dead Indian back there a ways."

Chavez didn't change expression. He didn't look at Owen at all.

Owen said, "You killed him, didn't you? You came this way last night."

Chavez glanced at him with surprised, injured innocence, and this, more than anything else, told Owen he had been right. He said, "Is that why you came along? Just to get where you could find Comanches to kill?"

Chavez shrugged. "What you talk about?"

Owen knew he ought to get rid of Chavez here and now. He ought to send him back. If the man refused, he ought to kill him like he'd kill a snake.

He also knew he wouldn't. They were shorthanded, so much that losing a man might mean the difference between making it to Abilene and not making it at all.

Angrily he said, "By God, at least get rid of

them. You want the whole damned tribe howling for our hair?"

Chavez didn't appear to have heard. Disgustedly, Owen turned and rode back along the flank of the herd.

A feeling that bordered on desperation touched him and stayed, growing stronger as he rode. He felt as though the lot of them were deliberately riding to their death.

Maybe they were, but they couldn't turn back now. To try would be to precipitate whatever crises were brewing in the minds of the men themselves.

He felt helpless and trapped. Disaster lay ahead but there was disaster, too, in trying to return.

☆ 10 ☆

THE incredible, grueling grind continued. Rain drove at them from out of the north, and for two days they lived in a sea of mud, soaked to the skin, and slept in soggy blankets that failed to keep them warm.

The cattle plodded along but when lightning flashed from the sky, they would start and halt nervously to stare around with frightened, rolling eyes. The men moved softly, and spoke softly, and made no sudden, sharp noises. And the cattle did not stampede.

But the intolerable strain took its toll on the dispositions of the men. The night the rain stopped, Chavez rose from the fire as Smith moved past him, unintentionally jostling the younger man and causing him to spill his coffee on the ground.

Smith's eyes flared and he flung the cup furiously away into the darkness. He swung, connected solidly with Chavez' cheekbone and sent him sprawling backward into the blazing fire.

Chavez rolled. He came up, his nine-inch knife in his hand. Except for his glittering eyes, his face was impassive and cold.

He moved toward Smith like a cat on his squat,

bowed legs. He held the knife before him and slightly below his waist. The cutting edge was up.

Smith yanked his gun from its holster. He backed, circling the fire as he did.

Owen came riding into the circle of firelight as Chavez rushed, having seen the start of it from a hundred yards away. The gun in Smith's hand barked, the sound echoing through the dripping, silent night.

The bullet missed. But Owen knew what the sound had done to the bedded herd. Without seeing them, he knew every one had leaped nervously to its feet. Trembling, ready, they waited only for a repetition of that sharp and unaccustomed sound.

Owen set spurs in his horses's sides. The animal leaped ahead, skidding in the churned-up mud.

Young Matt leaped out of his way, eyes wide and full of sudden fright. Owen caught a glimpse of Kate's white face staring out from the rear of the wagon. Then the shoulder of his horse hit Smith and knocked him sprawling in the mud.

Owen left his horse at the moment of impact, driving out of the saddle at Smith. He scrambled through the mud, groping with muddy hands for the gun.

He felt it, lost it, and groped for it again. Smith brought up a knee that caught Owen in the belly and drove the breath from him. But he kept fighting, trying, reaching for that gun. If it discharged again, the cattle would run. They'd be lost in the dripping darkness and the whole night, the whole day tomorrow would be spent in trying to gather them up again. Nor could they ever find them all.

He seized the gun a second time, wrenched it from Smith and flung it away into the night. He scrambled to his feet.

Smith rushed him recklessly. Owen stepped aside and sledged him on the side of the neck.

Chavez moved in behind him, heading for Smith, the knife still in his hand. Owen whirled, yanking his gun from its holster. He said through tight-clenched teeth, "Come on, you son of a bitch! Only I won't miss."

He had fought Smith recklessly to keep him from discharging his gun. Now he threatened to use his own. The threat of certain death was the only thing that would stop Chavez.

Chavez halted, stared at him with smoldering eyes for several moments from a distance of less than a dozen feet. Then, shrugging, his face as impassive as before, he thrust the knife back in its shealth.

Owen turned to glare at Smith. "You fire that gun once more and I'll take it away from you and ram it down your throat. You'll ride unarmed."

Smith got up, ineffectually trying to wipe his muddy hands on the equally muddy legs of his pants. "That Injun bastard will knife me while I sleep."

Owen said, "He might. But if he does, I'll blow his guts out."

He walked disgustedly to the fire. He got a cup and poured it full of coffee. He gulped it greedily. When he had finished, he said, "Smith you and Chavez get on out and relieve Tilton and Quade."

They glared at him sullenly. Again the peculiar certainty that they would never reach Kansas with this herd touched Owen. He would be smarter to call it off, to leave the cattle, take Matt and Kate and ride back south. Let Tilton and Quade and Smith and Chavez kill each other fighting over the herd.

He scowled blackly at the pair as they mounted

and rode on out. There would be more quarrels, more senseless fights over incidents as small as the one that had caused this one. He couldn't prevent them they were a natural outgrowth of exhaustion, tension, frustration and fear. But perhaps he could keep someone from getting killed. At least, he would have to try.

Not that he gave a damn about any of the men. His own exhaustion and worry had its own effect, that of making him hate and despise these men with whom he rode—with the possible exception of Quade. But he needed all four of them. He had to have them to drive the herd.

Quade and Tilton came riding in from the direction of the herd. Quade came to the fire and spread his hands to it. He was shivering from the cold and wet. His face looked older, more drawn than it usually did. He was an old man; the strain of the past few days had made this more noticeable than it usually was. Owen Scobey wondered briefly if Quade would live to see the end of the drive.

Tilton also came to the fire and backed up to it. Owen watched while Kate filled a plate with boiled beef for each of them. She got cups for them and they poured their own coffee. They ate standing because there was no place dry enough for them to sit down.

Finished, they carried their plates and cups to the wagon and dumped them into the wreck pan. Quade came back to the fire and began to pack his pipe. He glanced up at the sky. "It's clearin'."

Nobody replied. Tilton had found a cigar someplace in his gear, a black, twisted, Mexican cigar. He lighted it and puffed nervously.

Quade stared across the fire at him malevolently. His eyes were without much expression but they glinted redly in the firelight. He said, "Y' know, you got quite a reputation down along the border and the Gulf Coast."

Tilton glanced at him suspiciously.

Quade lighted his pipe deliberately before he went on. "Uh huh. Quite a reputation. Some say you've kilt yourself sixteen men."

Still Tilton did not reply. He stared unwinkingly at Quade.

"Some say they was all fair fights—self-defense, y' might say. But there's some—"

Tilton said harshly, "Get to the point, old man."

"I'm gettin' there. I was just goin' to say, there's others that claims you're a dirty yellow dog, that every one of them sixteen men was shot right square in the back."

Tilton's face congested with blood. His body tensed and his eyes blazed. Owen said sharply, "Shut up, Quade! For Christ's sake, ain't we got enough trouble around here without you tryin' to stir up more?"

"I ain't stirrin' up trouble. 'T wasn't me that said he shot them men in the back. How 'n hell would I know, except for what I've heard?"

Tilton made an obvious effort to control himself. Quade persisted, "Only what I've heard. But mebbe you c'd set me straight."

Tilton spoke from between clenched teeth. "I'll set you straight, all right, you mouthy old bastard!"

Quade pretended not to notice the threat, and ignored the epithet. "Appreciate that," he murmured. "They was one now, one of them killin's I'd like to know about."

Owen listened intently. Perhaps the reasons for Quade's obvious hatred of Tilton would now come out. He felt his muscles tense and knew that this discussion could explode violently without any warning at all.

" 'T was down in Sonora, it was. Memme you c'd put a number to this one but I couldn't, not knowin' about all the ones that went before."

A tiny frown touched Tilton's forehead. He stared intently across the fire at Quade. Matt stood to one side, white-faced, obviously scared at the undercurrents flowing so dangerously between the two.

Quade paused to get a blazing stick and relight his pipe. He cleared his throat. "Mexican, this one was. Feller named Jaramillo. 'Bout twenty, I reckon. They claim you wanted Jaramillo's woman an' kilt him for her."

Tilton's face had lost some of its congestion. It was almost pale. He growled, "What's it to you, old man? What do you care?"

"Care?" Quade stared at him with exaggerated innocence. "I don't care. I didn't know Jaramillo or his woman, either."

"Then why the talk, old fool?"

"Curiosity, y' might say. They say Jaramillo didn't even have a gun. Only a knife like all them greasers have. A gun against a knife, they say. Even the ones that hate you worst say you shot this one from in front. Only, the knife never got out of its sheath."

"You're a damn liar! He had that knife drawn back to throw!" Tilton stopped suddenly. His expression revealed that he had suddenly realized Quade's taunting had achieved the purpose for which it was intended. He said threateningly, "And what do you think, you damned old goat?"

"Me? Why, I reckon it's exactly like you say. I wouldn't call you a liar. I was just tellin' what folks down there say about—"

"They lie!"

"Sure they do. Sure." Quade's voice was sympathetic now.

Tilton glared at him steadily for several moments. Then he whirled and stalked away into the darkness, dragging his horse impatiently behind.

Owen said, "What the hell are you trying to do, Quade?"

"Do? I don't reckon I know what you mean."

"Did you know Jaramillo? Or his wife?"

"Never seed 'em in my life."

"Then why . . . ?"

Quade smiled faintly, his eyes on the leaping flames. But he did not reply.

He was getting Tilton's goat, all right. He was coming out into the open now and Owen knew instinctively that tonight only marked the start of Quade's campaign. He was willing to bet that Quade knew the details of each of the sixteen killings Tilton was supposed to be responsible for. And he was also willing to bet that Quade would bring them up, one by one, just as he had brought the first one up tonight.

He asked, "How long you been on Tilton's trail?"

Quade turned his head and stared steadily at him. "Don't reckon I know what you mean, Scobey. I ain't on Tilton's trail."

"How come you know so much about him, then?"

Quade's leathery face twisted. "I admire the man, Scobey."

"The hell you do! You hate him like a rattler hates water."

Quade shrugged. He was silent for several moments and then he said, "You're the one that hates him, Scobey. Why?"

Owen growled, "My business."

Quade nodded deliberately. "Just so. Same as my reasons are my business."

"You do hate him, then?"

Quade neither affirmed nor denied this. But at last he said, so softly that Owen scarcely heard, "The son of a bitch ain't never goin' to get to Abilene alive!"

☆ 11 ☆

MORNING dawned bright and clear and the land steamed under the hot rays of the morning sun. By nine o'clock, they were traveling no longer in mud but on firm, damp ground.

Yet, in each formerly dry stream bed, a raging torrent of thick brown water raced, rolling boulders along the bottom, carrying sticks and snags and even the dead, dry trunks of trees.

Fording these raging streams required time and effort, and the strain of it took its toll from each man in the small trail crew. Kate and Quade both left the wagon and helped, yet in spite of this additional help, night came and found them less than seven miles from their starting point. It also left the men too exhausted to quarrel. They hit their blanket rolls as soon as supper was finished and did not stir except when called to take their turn at night-herding duty.

Tonight, Owen switched them around, putting Chavez with Tilton, Quade with Smith. He took a shift with Matt himself because the boy solemnly insisted on doing his share.

In the morning, Smith disappeared. He was there

when Owen rolled out before dawn. He was gone when it was time to eat.

Owen cursed savagely under his breath. "Anybody see Smith leave?"

Quade nodded, his mouth full of boiled beef. "I did. I thought he was headin' out to the herd. Maybe that's where he is."

Tilton shook his head. "I just came from there. He ain't out there."

Owen growled, "If he'll desert one place, he'll desert another. But by God, he'd better not come back. He finished his coffee and tossed cup and plate into the wreck pan at the wagon. He stared at Kate. "Think you can drive?"

"Of course I can drive." Her eyes lingered on his face and turned soft. "You look so tired. I'm sorry I insisted on this."

Owen rubbed his bearded cheek. "Bit late for sorry," He regretted that almost as soon as he spoke and added quickly. "No need to say that. Not your doin', anyhow."

"What isn't?"

"Reason I came along."

"Can we make it without Smith?"

"We'll make it, Quade can take his place."

He stared at her a moment more. Her face was drawn, but it was somehow older, too. Her eyes seemed larger, her mouth softer than before. He watched her steadily until she looked away.

He went back to the fire. "Quade, you'll drive the horses. Kate can drive the wagon by herself."

Quade nodded and swung to the back of his horse. He headed out toward the horses, rope-corraled a quarter mile away.

Owen mounted his own mud-spattered horse. His clothes were so stiff with crusted mud that they had chafed him raw in a dozen places. He rode out toward the herd, and as he crested a small rise, he saw a column of troopers approaching about a mile away.

And suddenly he understood Smith's disappearance. The man had seen the troops before anyone else did. He had simply disappeared until they had passed and would probably be back as soon as they had gone.

The others came out behind him and started the herd trailing north. Owen rode to meet the group.

Richards was at their head, one of his lieutenants beside him. The leg of his trousers was slit and a bloodstained bandage showed beneath. The lieutenant carried his arm in a sling.

Nor were they the only casualties. Others along the line of ragged, exhausted men bore similar evidence of wounds.

Owen nodded. Richards raised an arm and halted the troop. They dismounted and collapsed to the ground. Most of them did not even look at Owen or at the herd a quarter mile away.

Richards dismounted stiffly and Owen followed suit. He said, "Captain, you look like you've had a hell of a time."

Richards grinned at him. "Take a look at yourself, Scobey. Take a look at yourself."

Owen rubbed his bearded dirty face. "Came to grips with 'em, did you?"

"We sure as hell did. We scattered them and drove what was left of them north. I doubt they'll be back for a spell."

"How far from here was this?"

"Fifty miles. I suppose." He sighed wearily. "We didn't have enough men. We had to abandon some of our wagons. And I have the uneasy feeling we've just been prodding a hornet's nest with a stick."

There was a long silence. Even Richards' men, resting on the ground, did not talk among themselves. At last, Richards glanced up. "How about you, Mr. Scobey? Looks like you've a good start toward what you set out to do."

"We're headed north." Owen grinned ruefully. "Beyond that, I'm damned if I know. We haven't enough men either. And they're fighting like stray dogs among themselves."

Richards peered closely at him. "We lost a man soon after we left you. Scobey. A man named Smith."

"That so? You figure he deserted or that a party of Indians caught him?"

"He deserted, Scobey." Richards' eyes were steady, penetrating. Owen met them steadily, knowing he was probably a fool for protecting Smith. Yet, he also knew that with one man less than he had right now . . .

Richards said, "Bad character. Due to be court-martialed on our return to the post." His face settled into an expression of distaste and he asked, "That girl—Miss Pryor. Is she with you on this drive?"

Owen nodded, a sudden uneasiness touching him.

"Then I suppose I had better tell you. Smith's accused of murder and rape. If we hadn't been so shorthanded, he'd never have been allowed to come along."

Owen was silent a moment. Then he asked, "You're sure about him? It isn't just a case of—"

"We're sure, Mr. Scobey. He'll be convicted and he'll be hanged. He had the girl's scratches all over his face and her blood all over his uniform." His expression of distaste deepened into outright revulsion. "She was only fourteen."

Owen said, "He was with us, Captain. Up until early this morning. We need him, but it'll suit me if you round him up and take him back to hang."

Richards nodded. "Figured he'd deserted to you. Wasn't any other place for him to go. But we didn't have time to stop and hunt him before. We still don't. My men are exhausted. Mr. Scobey. I've got to get them back to the post, where they can get medical attention. I'll lose half a dozen of the most seriously wounded if I don't."

Owen protested, "You can't just—"

Richards smiled wearily. "We can and we will, Mr. Scobey. I can't take time to hunt for him. My suggestion to you would be to turn him over to the authorities in Abilene. They'll send him back to us."

"And until then?"

"Watch him. Watch him close."

Richards turned to his horse. "Good luck, Mr. Scobey." He nodded to a sergeant behind him and the man's voice roared back along the line. "Prepare to mount!"

Richards swung to his horse and his lieutenant followed suit. Looking down at Owen, he said, "We broke up the main band of Indians, but there are still a lot of small parties around. They can cause you trouble."

The sergeant roared, "Mount!"

Owen nodded with bitter cynicism. He said, "Good luck, Captain," and watched the captain ride on south, followed by his straggling, weary troop. The supply and ammunition wagons followed, raising a long trail of dust from ground that had so recently been a sea of mud. They were loaded now with wounded instead of with ammunition and supplies.

He turned back toward the strung-out herd. If Smith returned immediately, Owen could still catch the troop and turn him over to them. But he knew, instinctively that Smith would not return today or probably tomorrow. He would not come back until he was sure Richards was too far south for the trip to be practicable or even possible.

Shrugging fatalistically, he took his place on the flank of the herd.

Smith did not return that day nor did he return the next. It was the third day after the encounter with Richards before he came riding into camp at sunup.

Owen stared at him sourly, contempt and anger in his eyes. "Figured it out just right, didn't you?"

Smith grinned. "I tried."

"Just because you don't go back with Richards doesn't mean you won't go back. I'll turn you over to the law as soon as we reach Abilene."

"He told you, then?"

"He told me."

Smith studied him a moment. He said, "It ain't true, Scobey."

"And the scratches? The blood?"

Smith's eyes were steady, startlingly candid. They mirrored injured innocence, but Owen thought he was overdoing it. "I was with a woman all right. Married woman. Her husband came home at the wrong time. She made out like I was forcin' her an' scratched hell out of me. Then the husband started in. It's a wonder I wasn't bloodier than I was, time I got away."

Owen nodded. "Maybe. I'm not a court-martial board. You tell them that."

"I will, Scobey. I will."

"In the meantime—" Owen eyes were suddenly as cold and hard as slate— "if I catch you talking to Miss Pryor or even looking at her . . . there won't be enough left of you to hang. Undertand?"

"I don't like threats, mister." Smith's air of innocence was gone. There was naked savagery in his eyes just now, an ugly turn to his mouth.

Owen's muscles tightened. "Take it up, then. Take it up right now."

Smith's features relaxed. "Not now, Scobey." He grinned recklessly. "Let's get a little closer to Abilene. A man might not make it alone from here."

"Then get on your horse and get to work."

Smith mounted and rode out in the direction of the horse herd. Owen watched him, watched the others follow. He began to help Kate clean up the camp and load the wagon.

The day was hot and still. Flies buzzed around the camp. There was a shine of perspiration on Kate's forehead. She had brushed her hair and it shone like satin.

Owen harnessed the team and hitched up for her. She smiled at him wearily. "Thank you."

"Uh huh." He walked to her and stood for several moments looking down, frowning. At last, he said bluntly, "Smith is dangerous. Watch out for him. The Army had him under arrest for murder and rape."

She nodded wordlessly. "I'll be careful. But you be careful, too. He will kill you if he can."

"I know." There was a lengthening silence between them. Owen knew he should mount up and ride out. But he didn't.

He said, "Kate . . ."

She glanced up at him. There was something—some unfathomed expression in her eyes. And suddenly his arms went out.

She was crying then, crying like a child in his arms. Her voice was muffled and choked. "I'm sorry. I'm a fool. We're not going to get to Abilene. We're not going to get anywhere. And it's my fault."

He tipped up her face. Her cheeks were wet with tears. Her mouth trembled.

He bent his head and kissed her on the mouth. And then her arms were around his neck, her mouth hungry and eager as though death were near.

He pulled back. He stared down into her face as though it was the last time he would see it, as though he were trying to memorize each feature of it. But his smile was sure. "We'll get there. We'll be all right."

She nodded, her eyes clinging to his face. Then, almost wearily, she mounted to the wagon seat. And Owen rode away.

The herd was half a mile north of the night's bed ground. Owen rode along in the dusty wake. He looked back once and saw Kate, straight and small and still on the wagon seat, as the creaking rig wound across the dusty plain.

His anger came slowly. But it grew as he rode along. Nothing was going to happen either to Matt or to Kate. He would kill every man in the crew if he must, but nothing was going to happen, to those two.

Matt was riding along slowly in the dust of the drag. Like that of Kate, his face was tired and drawn. He glanced at Owen and grinned.

Owen asked, "All right?"

"Sure." Matt straightened up. The way he sat his saddle, the set of his thin shoulders, the way his head cocked slightly to one side—these things were instantly reminiscent of Tilton.

Owen's face clouded. A boy needed a hero—someone to admire and emulate. That someone had been Owen until a month ago. Now it was Tilton.

The man had done his work. He had Matt admiring him. The rest was all downhill as far as Tilton was concerned.

Another new fear entered Owen's mind. If Tilton did tell the boy, it was certain now that Matt would refuse to remain with Owen anymore. Where then, would he go?

Owen's mind supplied an immediate answer to that. It was part of Tilton's plan that the boy should go with him. Not because he wanted him but because, admiring him, Matt would want to be like him.

So it wasn't altogether a matter now of Matt's love and respect for Owen. It was a matter involving the whole course of the boy's future life. Whether he would be a killer like Tilton or an honest man depended on whether Tilton told him about Owen or not. Tilton's hold over Owen was as great as it could ever be.

☆ 12 ☆

THIS day passed and so did the next. On the third day after Smith's return, Owen rolled out of his blankets, stared toward the west where the horse herd should have been and saw nothing but empty plain.

With a sinking feeling in his belly, he glanced hurriedly around in all directions. He swung to the back of his horse, rode to the top of a small knoll, the highest point in the vicinity, and scanned the horizons again. The horses were gone.

He returned to camp at a gallop. He'd taken a chance, a deliberately calculated one, in leaving the horses rope-corralled at night without a guard. Until now, the chance he'd taken had paid off. But last night, because there was no guard, the Comanches had run the horses off.

Coming into camp, he yelled, "Chavez! Tilton! Mount up and come on. We've got to get those horses back!"

Now the practice of keeping their horses near at hand all night paid off. At least, no one was afoot. They had mounts with which to follow the trail of the stolen horses.

Owen nodded to Chavez as they left the confines

of the camp, and Chavez rode ahead, eyes fixed steadily on the ground. Not that the horse herd would be hard to trail. But Owen had to know, and quickly, too, how many Indians were involved. If it was a large bunch, he'd have to take every man he had. If it was not, Tilton and Chavez would suffice.

Chavez quartered back and forth, across the trail pounded into the prairie sod by the bunch. After several minutes, he returned to Owen.

All three were riding at a steady lope. Chavez ranged up beside him and yelled, "Two hours!" He held up three fingers.

Owen nodded. Thereafter, they rode in silence, sparing their horses not at all. If they didn't catch the Comanches today, they wouldn't catch them at all because the Indians could travel all through the coming night, while they could not.

Chavez rode on Owen's right, a peculiarly intent expression on his face. His eyes were narrowed but they were very bright. His mouth was tightly compressed, as always, but every once in a while, Owen could see the corners twitch. He reminded Owen of a hungry, hunting animal on the hot trail of prey.

Tilton, on Owen's left, traveled without noticeable enthusiasm. To him, as to Owen, this was simply a necessary thing, neither enjoyed nor particularly disliked. It was one of the things a man had to accept.

Owen rode with a worried frown on his face. He was concerned that they would not catch up with the thieving Comanches in time. But he was also troubled about something else—about Smith back there in camp with Kate. About whether Quade would be sufficiently on guard to keep the man from killing him and taking Kate.

He should have brought Smith along and left Tilton back in camp. He simply had not thought of it in time and it was too late now.

Anyhow, for this job, he needed the best men he had. Without horses, the drive was doomed.

For a dozen miles, the trail led straight to the west, across blistering stretches of near-bare ground, skirting impenetrable thickets of mesquite, up shaly, crumbling trails to the top of gray sandstone bluffs, and on again across a sea of waving grass.

A fast trail. The horses had been forced to run, and made to continue even after they were winded and wanted to stop.

Owen's eyes narrowed against the dust, against the hot, dry wind, against the glare of the sun, trying to see a wisp of rising dust against the shimmering horizon.

But the hours passed, the miles dropped behind, and yet he saw nothing ahead.

At a dry stream crossing, he stopped and motioned for the others to do the same. His horse's neck and shoulders were flecked with foam. All three of their mounts stood trembling and breathing hard.

Owen glanced at Chavez. He pointed at the trail. "Are we gaining or losing ground?"

"We gain. A little."

"How far ahead?"

"One hour. Mebbe a little more."

Owen nodded briefly. He could form his own estimate of the Indians' goal. A village, lying somewhere to the west, that was much too large for three men to attack. When the Comanches reached that village, they would be safe. But until they did . . .

He lifted his horse to a trot, then to a lope again. The others followed suit.

Owen studied Chavez' face for an estimate of

their chances and decided they were good, for the peculiar intentness remained in the man's still face; the eager shine remained in his slitted eyes.

Chavez didn't give a damn about either the horses or the ultimate success of the drive, Owen thought. His interest was in catching the Comanches, in killing them, in satisfying the cancerous hatred of all Comanches that festered in his soul.

Realizing how urgent was the man's desire to catch the thieves, Owen let him set the pace. An Indian, even a man only part Indian, learned to measure the remaining strength of a horse against the miles remaining to be traveled. He had seen cases—had heard of others—in which an Indian or half-breed would reach his goal only to have his horse drop dead under him before he could dismount.

The sun hung in the western sky, a ball of molten brass. Heat waves rose from the blistering land. The three rode on.

Two hours before sunset, Chavez raised an arm and silently pointed ahead. Narrowing his dust and glare-reddened eyes, Owen stared.

Dust was there, a thin haze of it but plainly visible once you knew exactly where to look.

Chavez speeded up the pace. Owen's horse faltered, stumbled, then began to run strongly again. Tilton rode grimly at Owen's side, his face a mask of dust and sweat. His eyes peered out as redly as Owen's did, and his mouth was a thin hard line.

Owen glanced again at Chavez, thinking, "You'll see Comanches killed today."

Rapidly they began to overtake the braves. The three were spread out, one on the right, one on the left, one in the lead, because horses, even more than cattle, will follow a leader even though he may earry a man on his back. Owen could make out the markings and colors of the Indians' mounts. The one on the right was black and white—a pinto. The one on the left was black. The lead horse seemed to be sorrel but Owen could not be sure because of the pall of dust.

A quarter mile, that narrowed swiftly now. The horses of the three in pursuit traveled at a steady run, but foam flecked their shoulders, necks and hips and their breathing was hard and noisy.

The Indians glanced behind often and when the range was but three hundred yards, they veered right and left, reluctantly abandoning the prize they thought they had successfully stolen from the whites.

Tilton veered to follow the Indians on the left. Owen glanced at Chavez, expecting him to veer right. But the man did not. His eyes were upon the Indian in the lead.

Owen therefore swerved right and pounded along in the fleeing Indian's trail of rising dust.

The Indians rode toward a bluff a quarter mile to the right of the horse herd. Owen kept his eyes on the man, not bothering to look behind. Tilton could be relied upon to catch the one he pursued. Chavez could similarly be relied upon. Owen's only worry was to catch this one, to kill him so that he could not make his way to the village and bring back help.

The Indian disappeared into an arroyo and did not reappear again.

Owen glanced to right and left, looking for dust. He saw it on the right, therefore confidently pounded through the thin brush cover along the edge of the arroyo and plunged down the precipitous bank into it.

Immediately, he understood the Indian's ruse. The brave had left his horse upon entering the arroyo, but the horse had gone on, still running, for a quarter mile or more. This dust was what Owen had seen.

The brave himself was standing with his back to the high arroyo bank. He held a short rifle in his hands.

Owen didn't even reach for his rifle. His hand shot to the revolver at his side. The gaping muzzle of the large-caliber gun the Indian held looked more than an inch across to Owen's startled eyes.

Owen's horse saw the Indian the instant that he drew and shied away just before smoke billowed from the gun. The bullet touched Owen's sleeve, twitched it briefly and struck the arroyo bank behind him, showering him with reddish dirt.

His own gun was in his hands as the Indian dropped the rifle, a single-shot weapon, and reached for the tomahawk in his belt.

Owen fired, plunged on past, fighting his terrified horse, whirled him and fired again.

The Indian was driven back against the bank. Dirt, loosened by the impact, cascaded over him from the lip of the arroyo above his head. He turned and flung his tomahawk as Owen fired yet again.

The tomahawk, made of a stone lashed with rawhide to a polished wooden handle, turned end over end and struck Owen squarely in the chest.

His breath was driven from him with a mighty grunt. He was flung from his horse as though by a giant hand, and his chest felt as though it were filled with red-hot coals.

He struck the ground on his rump, gun still in his hand. He automatically thumbed the hammer back, his eyes on the Indian, who still had not fallen. Painfully Owen struggled to his feet.

But the Indian was dead. Pinned against the arroyo wall by his own weight, he fell only when his legs buckled and gave beneath him. He sat down on the floor of the arroyo as though he were very tired. He fell forward. His face buried itself in the blistering dust. His chest was still.

Owen eased the hammer of the revolver down, reloaded and slid it back into its holster. He put a hand to his chest gingerly, went over and stirred the Indian with the toe of his boot.

The man fell sideways and stared at the brassy sky with dead and empty eyes.

Owen looked up, searching for his horse. He walked down the arroyo two hundred yards before he caught the animal, standing now with heaving sides and drooping head. He mounted and rode back to the sloping place he and the Indian had used to enter the arroyo. He climbed his horse out to the level plain.

The herd had stopped and the horses were grazing, spreading out. Owen took down his rope and shook a loop in it.

Slowly, cautiously, he approached a black standing fifty yards from the rest of the herd. At fifty feet, he spurred his horse and his rope went out. It settled over the head of the black.

The animal's plunging stopped as he hit the end of the rope. He stood there trembling, rolling his eyes at man and horse.

Owen dismounted. He transferred his bridle and saddle to the fresh horse and turned the other loose. The animal immediately lay down, and rolled. Maybe he wasn't as played out as he had seemed, Owen thought.

He mounted the fresh horse. He circled the bunch at a gallop, started them back in the direction they had come. There wasn't much time left but there was enough to make half a dozen miles. If the stars were bright, they might even travel all through the night.

He had gone about a mile when he spotted Tilton coming toward him from the south. He scanned the horizon, but saw no sign of Chavez.

Tilton rode to him. Owen said, "Get him?"

Tilton nodded. "Yours?"

"Uh huh. Wonder where Chavez is."

Tilton shrugged. He shook out his rope, rode closer to the bunch and caught himself a fresh mount. He dropped behind to change his bridle and saddle. After several moments, he caught up again, riding the fresh horse now.

Owen had his own idea of where Chavez was. He'd caught his man, all right. But he hadn't been content to kill him quickly as Owen and Tilton had. He was back there now, devising some slow and painful way for the Indian brave to die. Or he had been killed himself. But somehow, Owen couldn't bring himself to believe that.

He scowled furiously as he rode along. All three of them had been near exhaustion this morning. They were closer to it now. And if they drove all night . . .

Furthermore, they would have to keep a guard on the horses after this. Next time, they might not be as lucky as they had been today.

The stars were bright and there was a crescent moon in the western sky that did not set until almost midnight. So they drove all through the night and arrived in camp as the sun was climbing out of the limitless western plain.

Quade sat on the wagon seat, his big buffalo rifle across his knees, while Smith built a fire of buffalo chips. There was a certain indefinable strain between the two that Owen instantly understood. But he said nothing. Quade had the situation in hand.

He waited until Smith had the fire going, then said harshly, "Get out there and stay with the horses, Smith."

Then man gave him a smoldering look, gave Quade another, then walked over and mounted his horse. Matt came from the wagon with Kate and the two glanced without much interest at Owen and at Tilton beyond.

They were tired, he thought, so tired they couldn't stir up much interest in anything. He asked, "Everything all right?"

They nodded in unison and he made himself grin at them. He felt as though he hadn't slept for a week. This drive had become almost more than human flesh could endure. But it had to go on because it wouldn't help a bit to stop. If Chavez was alive, he would catch them when he could.

☆ 13 ☆

OWEN rode point that day until Chavez returned in midmorning and took over the job. As the man rode up, Owen scowled at him and asked angrily, "What took *you* so damned long?"

Chavez shrugged and his face closed in on his thoughts. He grunted something surly and indistinguishable and Owen knew it was all he'd ever get out of the man.

He dropped behind to the flank, where Quade rode. "Damned breed," he growled. "I'll bet he left that brave staked out someplace without a tongue."

Quade nodded. "Likely did."

"And if he's found . . ." Owen didn't finish. All morning he had been seeing Indian signs. Maybe Richards had chased the main bunch north but there were a lot of small parties around. War parties, not hunting parties. The one he'd killed had been wearing paint.

He said, "Take over the drag from Matt. Tell him to go to the wagon and get some sleep."

Quade nodded and rode away. Owen watched as he approached Matt. He saw them talk briefly, saw Quade continue on toward the wagon, half a mile on the right of the slow-moving herd.

Thereafter, he watched the boy for a long, long time. Sometimes he was wholly obscured by dust. Owen knew how tired he was, knew the boy was ready to drop. But he'd refused the rest Quade had offered him and because he had strong pride stirred in Owen's heart. He turned and rode along the flank of the herd, feeling less tired himself, less angry and irritable than he had before.

But not less worried. There was an explosion near at hand, nearer than the railhead at Abilene. If the Indians didn't group and attack the herd, the explosion would come from the edgy tempers of the drovers themselves. All of them were near the breaking point.

After leaving Matt, Quade rode toward the wagon, then apparently changed his mind and rode up the right flank of the herd toward Tilton. He drew up beside the man and Owen could see them talking. After several moments, Tilton halted his horse.

Even at this distance, Owen could see Quade's teeth flash as he grinned at Tilton. Deliberately Quade turned his back and rode away toward the wagon, which was moving along slowly to the right of the herd and behind.

Tilton stared after him until he was several hundred yards away. Then he whirled his horse and rode recklessly after a handful of steers that had strayed too far from the main herd. Every movement he made was eloquent of anger and Owen realized Quade had been taunting him again.

He hoped Quade realized he couldn't go much farther with the man. Tilton would kill him if he was pushed much more. He'd kill him even if Quade refused to fight.

About four in the afternoon, they reached a valley between two high sandstone bluffs, a valley where grass grew deep, where a narrow stream wandered along, where there were a few stunted trees and dead ones for firewood.

Because of the nature of the place, it was ideal for stopping a couple of days. Two men could guard both the cattle herd and the horses. The remainder could rest and sleep.

He rode ahead and motioned Chavez back. Then he rode to the wagon and yelled at Quade to stop and make camp.

The cattle stopped of their own accord, gulping the rich grass hungrily. Owen waited until the men came in and then he said, "Quade, you and Smith take the first watch, one at each end of the valley. We'll stay here a couple of days and see if we all can't get some sleep."

Matt helped Kate build the fire and get supper going. Owen and Tilton and Chavez squatted numbly on the ground and waited.

There was something dangerously touchy about them all. But that would change, Owen hoped, once they'd had some sleep.

Tilton stared at him out of reddened angry eyes. "Keep that old fool off my back, Scobey, or I'll kill the son of a bitch. I've taken all I'll take from him."

"I'll talk to him."

"You'd better do more than talk. I mean it. I've stood all I'm going to stand from him."

Owen growled, "Damn it, I said I'd talk to him. Now shut up about it."

"Don't tell me to shut up, you bastard!" Tilton pushed himself abruptly to his feet. His face was a mask of dust and sweat. His lips were blackened with crusted dust and were drawn back until his teeth showed through. His right hand was like a claw six inches from the dusty butt of his gun.

Owen said, "Sit down and shut up."

Tilton's voice rose. "God damn you, get on your feet! I've stood all I'll stand from you, too!"

Owen stared up at him wearily. His anger was rising dangerously and he tried, without success, to fight it down. He realized suddenly how much he hated this man standing before him and daring him to fight. He realized how badly he wanted that fight.

He didn't really care any more how the fight came out. He didn't stop to realize or even think how fast Tilton was with that gun of his.

He pushed himself stiffly to his feet. He wanted to draw his gun and shoot it out with Tilton. He was ready to do just that.

He heard Kate's voice, alarmed and scared. "Stop it! Stop it, you hear?"

He glanced quickly toward her, saw her widened, frightened eyes, saw young Matt's scared, drawn face behind her.

And he realized that if he fought Tilton with guns, they'd both probably end up dead. Which would doom the drive and leave Kate and Matt out here with only Quade to care whether they lived or died. Quade, who was old and tired and no match either for Chavez or for Smith.

On the point of snatching his gun from its holster, Owen changed his mind, not about fighting Tilton but about the way it must be done.

He dived at Tilton's legs, felt his shoulder strike them as Tilton's gun discharged inches above his head.

The man staggered back and fell, and Owen clawed along the ground like some savage animal until he felt his hands close on Tilton's wrist, the one that held the gun.

He wrenched with savage brutality, wanting to break Tilton's arm if he could. Tilton howled, released the gun and brought his left hand around to claw at Owen's face and probe there for his eyes.

Owen turned his head, released Tilton's wrist and brought both hands up to close around the man's throat.

Tilton doubled frantically. His knee dug ruthessly into Owen's groin, sending pains shooting upward through his belly. He released Tilton's throat and smashed his fists, one after the other, into the hatred-twisted face. He saw Tilton's nose spurt blood, felt his teeth crack under the second blow.

Then they were rolling, growling and snarling like fighting dogs instead of men, but completely savage, both of them.

Gouging, kneeing, clawing, they rolled across the clearing and against the wagon tongue. Tilton seized his hair and beat his head against the weathered surface until Owen felt his senses fade and reel.

His hands went up and closed around Tilton's throat, the thumbs digging savagely in, closing the man's windpipe until he couldn't breathe. His grip on Owen's hair relaxed and broke and his hands seized Owen's wrists to try and break his hold.

Owen rolled, and now began to beat Tilton's head against the ground. His face was a mask of dust and blood and undiluted fury. All of Tilton's threats came flooding back, the fear and helplessness he'd felt in the face of them.

His hold on Tilton's throat broke. His fists smashed with ugly regularity into the man's congested and contorted face.

There was no consciousness in Owen that he was slowing down. He seemed to be moving as quickly, striking as hard as he had at first. Yet his arms felt like lead and in reality moved with deliberate slowness.

Tilton rolled him off with a mighty heave and climbed up the wagon wheel until he stood erect. He turned to face Owen, his chest heaving with exertion, his breath choking in and out of his lungs with a sound like a horse rasp trimming a horse's hoof.

Owen, having risen without the help of the wagon, lunged at him and smashed him, first in the belly, then in the face as the first blow doubled him. As Tilton began to fall, Owen sledged him again on the back of the neck.

Tilton collapsed face downward in the dust. He began to crawl and Owen watched him, head hanging, breath coming painfully and in short, quick gasps.

He understood Tilton's intention just as the man reached his objective—his saddle—and seized the stock of his rifle, protruding from the boot.

Owen felt as he sometimes had in dreams. He felt rooted to this spot, unable to move, unable to do anything but watch death rush at him.

Then he realized he was halfway to the man there on the ground. As Tilton yanked the gun clear of the saddle scabbard, Owen reached him and kicked out savagely with a dusty, booted foot.

The boot struck the rifle first, knocking its muzzle aside. The receiver hit Tilton in the mouth with a sharp and audible crack.

Owen kicked again, knowing that if he tried to stoop and seize the gun, he would fall on his face.

This time, his boot toe connected with Tilton's throat. The man began to choke and gasp, bent and laid the gun flat on the ground as he tried with both hands to support himself.

Owen put his foot down on the gun, with his weight holding it securely against the ground. He kicked again with the other foot, connected with Tilton's ribs. The man groaned, released the rifle and rolled aside.

Owen's voice was like a file. "Chavez, come and get this gun."

He stepped off as Chavez stooped to pick it up. He stared at Tilton, half conscious on the ground.

He had never been this tired in his life before. He felt a presence beside him, glanced aside and saw Kate standing there, a dipper of water in her hand.

He took it from her and gulped it down, spilling half of it over his chin and throat and chest. He handed it back and looked down into her face.

He saw there a terrible kind of shock. He saw pity and he saw outrage. But he saw something else as well, so closely hidden behind the other things as to be very easily missed.

It was not approval, nor was it love. It was trust, and faith, simple dependence upon his judgment and his strength.

He staggered to the wagon, took down a bucket and dipped it in the water barrel. He raised it and poured it deliberately over his head.

Cold by contrast to the air, it shocked him immediately into full consciousness again.

He leaned against the wagon, his knees like water, and waited for his breathing to become normal again.

Tilton tried to get up once more. He got as far as his hands and knees. Then he collapsed to the ground and lay completely still. His breathing was harsh and noisy, as though he were asleep.

And now Owen did the thing he had been dreading. He looked at Matt.

The boy was watching him with steady, widened eyes. Such a mixture of emotions were there in his expression that Owen could make out little but the confusion of them.

The boy switched his glance to the unconscious man on the ground. And briefly Owen saw anger in his eyes, and pity, and disappointment, too. He glanced back at Owen and only the anger showed. "Why'd you have to do that to him? Why'd you have to hurt him so bad?"

Owen said softly, "He'd have killed me, boy."

Confusion touched young Matt's face again. Tears welled up into his eyes. His mouth began to work helplessly.

He whirled suddenly and ran. Before he was out of sight, Owen could hear the tortured sobs racking him, the wordless cries of a boy in torment.

Exhaustion was contributing to his hysterics. But it wasn't only exhaustion.

Matt had given Tilton a part of the loyalty and respect that previously only Owen had possessed. He was torn between the two and would be torn until one of them was dead.

☆ 14 ☆

Owen slept as though he were dead all through the night, unaware that Kate and Matt took over the early-morning watch from Smith and Quade. Nor did fear of Tilton trouble him. He knew that in spite of Quade's accusations, Tilton lived by his code. Never kill an unarmed man. Never shoot one in the back.

But he dreamed, mixed-up nightmares about howling savages screaming in to attack, about a shoot-out with Tilton on the street of a flimsy frontier town, about catching Smith attacking Kate and tearing him apart with his hands, only to finish and find Kate dead.

He woke, sweating, muttering indistinguishably. The sun was beating straight into his eyes. He sat up and stared around, then relaxed and rubbed his eyes.

Smith and Quade were gone. Tilton and Chavez were sleeping still, Tilton snoring noisly, Chavez as silent as an animal. Matt was sleeping, too, but Kate was awake, sitting beside the fire, looking at him with serious unsmiling eyes.

He said, "Good morning. Looks like I slept pretty late."

"You needed it."

"Uh huh." He glanced up at the sun, guessed from its position that it was almost ten o'clock. He must have been exhausted. He hadn't slept late in years.

"Coffee?"

He got up, shaking his head. "I'm going to get clean first." He stumbled to the wagon, found his duffel bag and rummaged in it until he found his razor, a change of clothes and a bar of laundry soap. Carrying them, he headed upstream. Finding a place where the water circled a dead tree and was better than knee deep, he stripped off his clothes and began to wash.

The water revived and fully awakened him. When he had finished, he lathered with laundry soap and shaved by feel. After that, he soaked and soaped his dirty clothes, washed them with efficiency born of practice and draped them over a snag to dry. He dressed, buckled on his gun and walked back into camp.

His lips were split from the fight last night. One of his eyes was swollen and probably black, he thought.

Matt was awake and looked more rested than he had in many days. But there was something withdrawn in his expression as he looked at Owen, something doubtful and wondering.

Owen went to the fire and poured himself a cup of coffee. He gulped it, then accepted the tin plate Kate handed him. He ate in silence until Kate asked, "How far do you think we've come? And how far have we yet to go?"

He shrugged. "Halfway, I guess. Pretty close to that. Near as I can tell, we're still in Texas but we ought to be hitting the Cherokee Strip pretty soon."

She said thoughtfully, "I wish now that we hadn't come. I'm afraid. . . ."

He said, "We came and we can't go back. We'll make it." He felt a touch of confidence for the first time in many days.

"How long are we going to stay here?"

"Today. Tonight. We'll go on tomorrow."

He heard Matt's voice, suddenly soft and scared. "Owen."

He glanced around at the boy. Matt was staring past him toward the top of the gray sandstone bluff lying to the south. Owen swung his head and stared in the same direction.

Up there, silhouetted against the morning sky, he saw an Indian sitting on his horse, staring down into the valley below. As he watched, another brave joined the first, and then another still. The three sat there motionless for several long moments, then turned their horses and rode slowly out of sight.

Kate asked worriedly, "What does it mean?"

"Nothing. There have been small parties around all along. We've seen their tracks, but this is the first time they've showed themselves."

"Why?"

"Are they showing themselves right now?" He tried to sound unconcerned. "Who knows how the mind of an Indian works? Wait until there are twenty in that bunch. That's time enough to start worrying."

He got up and walked to his horse. He mounted, rode out of camp. At the edge of the horse herd, he roped himself a fresh mount, changed bridle and saddle, then put the horse up the rocky slope leading to the top of the southern bluff.

He rode cautiously, watching both the ground and

the surrounding hillsides. When he reached the top, he circled until he cut their trail.

He had seen three. But he found tracks of eight horses leading off toward the west.

Frowning, he returned toward camp. In spite of what he had told Kate, he was worried about the sudden appearance of the braves. He knew they wouldn't bother to follow the herd unless they wanted something.

Horses? It was possible. Scalps? That was possible, too. But if they wanted either horses or scalps, he doubted if they'd have shown themselves. They would have struck without warning at dawn some day. They'd have attacked the camp or run the horses off before the drovers even knew they were around.

Chavez? That made the most sense of any guess so far. They probably wanted Chavez but were not yet ready to attack the camp for him.

Owen rode back slowly. He changed directions before he reached camp and rode downstream to the far edge of the grazing herd.

Quade was sitting his hip-shot horse in the morning sun, puffing comfortably on his pipe. He watched Owen approach, grinned and said, "It's an improvement."

Owen rubbed his clean-shaven jaw, then gestured with his head toward the southern ridge. "See 'em?"

Quade nodded. Owen said, "There were eight. What do *you* make of it? You know the Comanches pretty well."

Quade puffed on his pipe a moment. "They could be after horses or they could be after scalps."

"But you don't think they are."

"Nope. You'd never see 'em if they was after either one."

"Chavez, then?"

"I figure so."

"Then what the hell are they waiting for?"

Quade frowned. "Reinforcements, maybe. An Injun likes the odds in his favor. He don't favor dyin' more 'n any other man. Or maybe their medicine ain't right." But he didn't sound convinced.

Owen said, "I'll send Chavez out to take your place. If you can get anything out of him, let me know."

Quade nodded and Owen rode back to camp. He was certain in his own mind now that soon they were going to have to cope with an Indian attack. Spread out, driving the herd, they'd have very little chance of surviving it. The Indians could pick them off one by one. As if they didn't have enough trouble inside the camp, they now had to face trouble from outside it.

Chavez was eating when he rode into camp. Owen said, "Soon's you finish, go take over for Quade."

Tilton approached from the direction of the stream, washed and shaved, but wearing the same clothes. Owen said, "Take Smith's place. Keep your eyes peeled. There's a war party hanging around."

Tilton stared angrily at him. His face was puffed and bruised even more than Owen's was and there was smoldering hate in his eyes. "Why bother warnin' me? You wish they would get me."

Owen nodded. "I do. But not right now. I can't spare you yet."

"You'd better hope they get me soon. Because next time you put a hand on me, I'm going to blow your insides out."

Owen scowled. "You just try that. Any time. But put the first one right between my eyes, because if you don't, you're dead. Now get out of here and take Smith's place unless you want to try it now."

He thought for a moment that Tilton would and realized that he didn't really care. He had lived with Tilton's threats too long. He had reached the point where he wasn't afraid, of this threat, anyway. Fighting it out with Tilton might solve a lot of things.

Tilton's eyes seemed even paler than usual and were as cold as winter ice. His thin mouth was thinner, and wider, and colorless and cold. Owen knew he couldn't match Tilton's draw. He also knew that unless Tilton's first shot robbed him of consciousness by striking him in the head, he would get off at least one shot that would hit its mark.

Tilton turned abruptly and strode away. Owen watched him until he had mounted and ridden out of sight.

After a while, Smith and Quade came in and promptly went to sleep. Kate climbed into the wagon and also slept. Owen stared thoughtfully at Matt, sleeping with his mouth open in the shade of the wagon. He glanced up at the southern ridge, but found it empty now.

One thing, he thought. The Comanches wouldn't kill the boy. They'd take him with them and raise him as one of their own.

But he'd better move this herd, and soon. Waiting here any longer would only give the Comanches more time for whatever it was they were waiting for.

Shortly after noon, therefore, they moved the cattle out, pointing them north again, pushing hard now to cover a day's distance in less than half a day.

And all day long, when Owen would look behind,

he would see the dust of the slowly pursuing braves. Like patient scavengers, they hung tenaciously on the drovers' trail.

The first day it was eight, the second ten. Four more joined the party on the third day and now they moved in closer, following a mile behind the drag of the herd.

Owen moved the wagon in until it was traveling less than a quarter mile to the right of the drag. He moved the horse herd closer, too, and he stayed farther back himself, nearer to Matt, who was plainly and unashamedly afraid.

It was like dying out on the plain, and watching the ugly buzzards circling close above your head, waiting only until the spark of life should go. It was like staring into the gaping muzzle of a gun, knowing it will go off and kill you but not knowing precisely when.

The Indians would attack when their number had grown enough. Or when the one they were waiting for arrived.

He was reasonably sure that the Comanches were after revenge. Chavez had probably caught and killed some Indian important enough to bring on such tenacity. A chief, perhaps, or the son of a chief. Perhaps even a medicine man.

And the Indians moved closer as their number increased. Twenty strong, they now were less than a half mile behind the herd.

Owen dropped back and rode along immediately beside young Matt. The boy was pale beneath his coat of dust and tan. He kept nervously licking his chapped and dusty lips. He looked behind, then at Owen. "What are they going to do? Why don't they do it?"

"They're waiting for something, boy."

"For what?"

Owen shrugged. "More Indians, maybe."

"What are we going to do? Just wait until they decide they've got enough?"

Owen kept his eyes on the land ahead. There was rough and rocky country there, ten or fifteen miles from here. If they could reach it, perhaps they could find someplace to make a stand. Perhaps they could work an ambush of their own and dispose of the Indian threat once and for all.

He said, "I figure to stop when we reach those hills. We'll try and ambush 'em. Until then, there's nothing much we can do but what we're doing now. You ride on up the flank, Matt. If they do move up, I want to be back here."

"I'll stay with you." Matt's eyes were steady and his mouth was firm in spite of the fright in his eyes.

"You do what you're told. I can shoot twice as fast as you. That's why I'm staying here."

Matt said, "Owen . . ."

"Yes?"

The boy licked his lips and fumbled visibly for words. At last, he said, "Nothing, I guess. Nothing."

A certain tightness was in Owen's throat as he watched Matt ride away. Right now he was prouder of the boy than he had ever been before. Matt had done a man's work all the way. A boy's fear was in him but he was controlling it like a man. And in spite of weariness and fear, he could still think of apology to Owen for liking a man Owen hated. For that was surely what had been on his mind just now.

Apparently sensing the urgency of doing so, Chavez stepped up the pace; Tilton, on the right, rode like a demon back and forth along the flank, urging the cattle along. Without being told, they all seemed to know that what little chance of survival they had lay in those rocky hills ahead.

Owen yelled and slapped his boot with the ends of the reins as he pushed the stragglers along. Often, he glanced behind, for he knew he could not afford to be surprised.

Confidently, the Indians rode in the wake of the herd. Steadily, if slowly, the distance between the herd and the rocky hills decreased.

The day seemed to drag. The sun seemed permanently painted on a spot in the sky. He could see Quade drawing the wagon in closer as the Indians drew closer behind. He could see Kate's straight figure on the seat beside him.

Why did the Indians wait? They could overwhelm the drovers now at any time they wished. Twenty against seven. Three-to-one odds. The drovers, spread out, would have no time to group or find cover for a stand.

It was not numbers, then, holding the Indians back. They were waiting for someone to join them. Only when he had, would they attack.

So Owen watched the horizons to the rear, to right and left. Perhaps he would see the approach of the one they were waiting for in time to set up some defense. Perhaps he could at least pull his men in to the wagon and make a stand from there.

Inexorably the sun slid down the western sky. Inexorably the line of rocky hills drew near. He could make them out clearly now, each ridge, each pile of rocks, each precipitous draw and ravine.

Glancing alternately behind and ahead, he pushed the cattle along. He saw one shallow draw, wide at first and steeply sloping up. There were high and barren hills on either side of it, hills so steep and rocky as to bar the passage of a horse.

He could not tell what lay beyond the crest. Right now it didn't matter anyway, because this was the only place that offered them any chance to fight off the impending attack.

He swung his head again. Far to the rear and on his right, he saw a rising cloud of dust.

He stopped his horse and peered more closely as the dust of the drag began to settle around him. He could see specks at the base of that approaching cloud of dust. He tried to count, but they were still too far away.

The time was here. By the time those swiftly traveling horsemen arrived, he had to have the herd headed up that long slope toward the rock-strewn pass. If he did not . . .

He yanked his gun and fired several shots into the air. He saw Matt turn his head, saw Tilton look back, saw Quade turn the wagon slightly so that he could look behind. He couldn't see Chavez or Smith because of the rising dust.

But those he saw immediately understood. Tilton pulled his revolver and emptied it into the air, howling like a maniac as he did. Matt pulled his rifle from its scabbard, fired, reloaded, fired again. Quade whipped the wagon team into a straining, lunging lope.

Behind the herd, the Indians stopped to wait for those galloping toward them from behind. The herd picked up speed and as they did, the cloud of dust they raised grew denser and rose higher into the air.

That low pass, those lifesaving rocks, looked as though they were a hundred miles away. Owen didn't know whether they'd make it in time or not.

☆ 15 ☆

An eternity. Rising dust now obscured everything from Owen's sight but the fifty or so head that were nearest him.

Riding back and forth, he let some of the weaker, slower ones fall behind, knowing it might soon be necessary to abandon the entire herd. Unless they found shelter, a vantage point, they would have no chance at all. If the cattle slowed them down too much, they'd all have to be left behind.

He coughed violently from the dust. His nostrils and throat seemed closed with it.

The cattle moved now at a lumbering trot. Like water, they poured into a wide, deep arroyo and flowed up and out on the other side, bawling, making a collective sound like thunder on a distant black horizon.

From here, the long ravine looked lower than it had before, and flatter, but he knew it was an illusion. It was high enough. It would have to be.

Looking back, he saw that the two groups of Indians were less than a quarter mile apart. He could count the newcomers now. There were eight. Which raised the odds to four to one. He cursed softly under his breath.

The first group rode to meet the eight. They joined forces, sat their horses, talking and gesticulating for several moments. Then they galloped in pursuit.

The last of the cattle ran down into the arroyo and Owen slid after them. The dust was so thick he couldn't see the far side of it less than fifty feet away.

He emptied his revolver and yelled like a maniac. He reloaded as his horse climbed out on the far side. He glanced behind again.

The Indians were like ghosts, dimly seen through the pall of yellow dust. He yanked his rifle from the boot and stepped out of his saddle to the ground. They were far too close. Before the herd was halfway up the slope, they'd have it surrounded and the men shot down. They had to be stopped, scattered. The drovers had to have more time.

Owen flopped behind a rock. Dragging the reins, his terrified horse went on, leaving him alone. He waited, sweating heavily, breathing harshly in the settling dust.

The Indians came on confidently, in a group. Owen rested his rifle on a rock and took careful aim. While they were yet two hundred yards away, he fired.

The horse of the one in the lead catapulted forward and tumbled end over end on the ground, throwing his rider almost thirty feet. Two horses of those following got fouled up with the falling horse and went down, too. The rest of the Indians pulled to a plunging halt and scattered like quail to right and left.

Owen fired again, carefully, and another horse went down. He was shooting deliberately at horses. They made a larger target in this pall of deceptive dust. Knocking them down slowed the pursuit even more effectively than if he had been hitting men.

Owen got up and backed away from the lip of the arroyo. He drew several shots from the Indians, turned and ran in the wake of the herd. He needed to find his horse and soon, or the Indians would pour across the arroyo, overtake him and kill him.

He peered into the settling cloud of dust. Damn, a horse that wouldn't stand! He continued up the rocky slope, his breathing becoming more ragged as he ran.

Glancing behind, he saw that the Indians had grouped again and were pouring into the arroyo. He speeded up his pace, stumbled and nearly fell. He had only a minute or two left. If he didn't find and catch his horse by the end of that time, he'd just have to turn and fight it out. He'd have to try and slow them enough to allow the drovers to reach the temporary safety of the top.

He glanced behind again. The first of the pursuing braves climbed his plunging horse out of the arroyo to level ground.

Owen stopped, panting heavily. He checked his revolver loads, shoved it back in its holster and stood spread-legged, waiting with his rifle in his hands.

A shout from behind . . . The sound of a horse's hoofs . . . "Owen! Where—"

He yelled, "Here!"

Matt came pounding toward him, dragging Owen's riderless horse behind. Owen ran, seized the reins and leaped astride. He flung a shot toward the Indians pouring up out of the arroyo, then whirled the horse, sank his spurs and thundered after Matt.

Matt had saved his life. Without a horse, caught here alone, he wouldn't have had a chance.

He knew how terrified the boy had been. He knew how much raw courage coming back had taken.

The pair thundered halfway up the slope before they overtook the tail end of the herd. Owen roared. "Tilton! Chavez! Smith!" He swerved to one side and raced up the flank of the herd.

He saw a horseman materialize out of the dust, another. He yelled, "Get down! Hold the bastards back!"

They swung to the ground and waited in the swirling dust for the Indians to appear. Owen yelled, "Matt! Where's the wagon?"

Matt had halted his horse. He was preparing to dismount and take his stand here with the men. He looked at Owen with confused and terrified eyes, then pointed. Owen yelled, "Come on!" and reined that way.

The wagon was bounding up the rough slope behind a straining, plunging team. Quade was standing, the reins in one hand, a long, braided whip in the other. Mercilessly he flayed the rumps of the terrified horses.

Kate sat on the seat beside him, holding on desperately with both hands. It seemed to Owen they'd both be flung clear by the rocking motion of the wagon, but miraculously they were not.

A trail of gear marked the wagon's path—water barrels, supplies, cooking utensils, firewood. Behind him, Owen heard the first sharp crackle of gunfire as the drovers opened up.

Running free, the cattle continued up the slope. Owen caught a brief glimpse of their leaders disappearing over the top. The wagon was almost to the top when he rode alongside and bawled, "Quade!"

He pointed toward a group of high boulders at

one side of the summit. Quade's face was a twisted mask and Owen wasn't immediately sure he understood. Then Quade turned the team and headed for the shelter Owen had pointed out.

Owen hauled his horse to a halt, looked around for Matt, saw him and yelled, "Go with them!"

Matt hesitated and Owen bawled, "Damn it, do as you're told!"

Matt whirled his horse and galloped after the wagon.

The dust was settling rapidly now that the cattle were gone. Through it he could see the Indians running up the slope toward the three men partially concealed behind low rocks.

He swung from his horse, this time holding onto the reins and staying on his feet. He snapped the rifle to his shoulder and fired as rapidly as he could into the oncoming ranks.

At this range, he could scarcely miss. He knocked down two before surprise at finding themselves in such a deadly cross fire sent them racing back down the slope.

Owen swung up and rode to the three he had stationed in the rocks. Tilton and Smith were getting up, but Chavez was still firing, intently and slowly, at the retreating braves. Three lay nearby on the ground, another farther down.

Chavez got up at last. He walked to one of the Indians on the ground, one who was still breathing, and brutally smashed his skull with the butt of his gun.

Owen didn't protest, thought the sight of it made his stomach churn. He yelled, "Come on," and led them to the summit. He pointed to a spot where the rocks were high and closely spaced. "Tilton. Chavez. Smith. In there."

He crossed the summit to where the wagon stood. He was relieved to see that one of the water barrels was still in place. Quade and Kate were under the wagon. Matt was tying his horse to the wheel.

Owen dismounted and tied his horse beside Matt's. The quiet now seemed as deafening as all the noise had been only moments before. His voice sounded loud and hoarse. "Matt . . . Thanks, boy. I'd have been dead if you hadn't come back."

Matt's gray face flushed with embarrassment but some of the fear went out of his eyes. Owen's hand touched his shoulder and gripped it.

He crawled under the wagon and Matt followed suit. Owen grinned at Quade. "You're a teamster. That was real driving."

Quade grinned back. "If a man's scared enough, he can do a lot of things. I was scared."

Kate, nearly in tears, said, "How can you two joke, when—"

She was near hysterics from fear and strain, nearer the breaking point than Owen had seen her.

He said, "See how much water we've got left. And see if there's any food."

She stared uncomprehendingly at him for a moment. Then she obediently got up and climbed into the wagon. Matt was beginning to tremble violently with delayed reaction. Owen said, "Unhitch the team, Matt. Lead them back a ways and tie them up."

The boy's trembling slackened. He got up and began to unhook the tugs. A few moments later, the wagon tongue dropped and Owen heard the team being led away.

He peered closely down at the empty slope. There was not an Indian in sight save for the dead ones lying there. At the bottom, across the dry arroyo, he could see the bodies of the horses he had shot. But nothing moved.

Quade asked, "Now what?"

"I guess we stay here and wait. We'll find out pretty soon what they want and how bad they want it."

"What if they want Chavez? You going to give him up?"

Owen didn't reply immediately. He knew there was only one answer he could make and never really considered any other. He shook his head.

"He's as much Indian as white."

"Yeah. But he's one of us." Even as he spoke, he knew that wasn't strictly true. Chavez' actions were more those of an Indian than a white. So was his way of thinking.

Owen guessed there was a matter of pride involved. In spite of the risk to the others in refusing them Chavez, there was nothing else he could do. To surrender him would be to earn the Indians contempt and probably a renewed and vigorous attack.

The sun was down behind the ridge at Owen's right and the slope before him was in shadow. Ridges and hills threw shadows on the plain beyond, creating a patchwork of alternate shade and bright sunlight.

The sky, the clouds drifting slowly along on a summer breeze, were stained with orange that deepened in color to gold even as he watched. Unless the Indians attacked immediately, they would probably wait until morning now. No Indians likes to fight at night.

Matt came back from tying the team and a few moments later, Kate came crawling under the wagon after him. She said breathlessly, "There's about a quarter of a barrel of water left. The cover came off and most of it splashed out. But we've plenty of food."

Light faded from the land, leaving it colorless before the coming night. More slowly but as surely, color faded from the clouds until all before them was drab, dull gray. The air cooled and cleared.

Owen crawled out from beneath the wagon. Staying out of sight, he walked among the rocks until he reached the summit of the ridge.

On this side, the land fell away, bare and almost flat for what seemed like a hundred miles. Even what grass grew was short and thin. A lizard couldn't approach unseen.

He stared beyond the slope to where the land flattened out. He saw the cattle out there, several miles away, scattered, beginning to graze. He saw the horse herd.

He turned and walked back toward the wagon. They were far from secure. The odds against them were still more than three to one. At dawn, the Indians would come creeping upon them from three directions, from right and left through the screen of boulders, from the south up the ravine. And while they would probably not come from the north, that direction still would have to be watched.

It was deep gray dusk, by the time he reached the wagon. He said, "Just as well rustle up some grub. It'll be a damn long night."

Kate came out from beneath the wagon, followed by Matt. Quade was already standing at the rear of it, peering down the slope toward the south. He said softly, "Wouldn't do that just yet. Here they come."

Owen whirled. They were barely visible in the fading light of dust, but already he could hear the dull pound of their horses hoofs.

He said, "Under the wagon!" and yelled across at the others, "Watch it! They're coming!"

Scarcely had his voice died out than rifle fire burst from the rocks at the other side of the ravine. Below, the Indians' voices raised in a yell that blended eerily until it sounded almost like the barking of coyotes on some distant ridge.

Quade's rifle roared. Kate was back under the wagon. So was Matt. The boy's rifle was poked out in front of him and it roared as Owen dived under the wagon.

He fired as rapidly as he could operate the action. When the rifle was empty, he flung it aside and yanked his revolver from its holster.

He had never heard of Indians fighting voluntarily at night. And while this wasn't strictly night just yet, it would be soon. Something mighty powerful must be prodding them. All they had to do was wait until tomorrow. . . .

Down there on the slope, the Indians were dropping. A horse went down, rolled on his rider and wrenched a high yell of pain from him. Across where the others were, rifles and revolvers barked like a string of firecrackers. Muzzle flashes blossomed on the slope.

Almost to the wagon, the line of riders broke, hesitated, then turned and galloped away in the direction they had come. One lay wounded, trying to crawl, between the wagon and the three across the flat ravine. With fingers he couldn't keep steady, Owen began to reload.

☆ 16 ☆

As he finished reloading his rifle, Owen heard sounds on his right. Yanking his head around nervously, he dimly saw Smith, Tilton and Chavez crossing the open space toward the wagon. One of them was hurt, being supported between the other two.

He muttered, "Damn it, I never heard of Indians fighting at night. I didn't think they would unless it was forced on them."

Quade grunted. "Depends on what they're fighting for. This outfit's after revenge."

"How do you know?"

"I savvy their lingo some. Made out some of what they were yellin' as they came up the slope."

"Chavez?"

"Uh huh. I only got snatches here an' there. But he's kilt the chief's son, near as I can guess, an' they want to give him the same treatment. They call him Short Legs."

The three had reached the wagon in time to overhear. Chavez was carrying a wounded leg. He crawled under the wagon, silent, occasionally grunting softly with pain. Owen slid out from under the wagon, saying, "I'll find something and fix that leg."

132

Quade, Kate and Matt followed him out. Smith said, "By God, I say let's give him up."

Quade's voice was contemptuous. "You should of given that one back to Captain Richards, Scobey, when he first came walkin' in."

Smith snarled, "What you so high an' mighty about, old man? Your life's all over with. You ain't even interested in women no more."

"You'd be a hell of a sight better off if you wasn't either, you yellow-bellied bastard!"

Owen said, "Shut up, both of you. We're not giving anybody up, I don't care what he's done. Not to the Indians, anyhow."

"Then what're we going to do?" Smith's voice was thin.

"Same as we've been doing up to now. Fight 'em off."

Smith insisted, "I say we take a vote. We oughta have something to say about whether we get killed or not."

Quade grunted savagely, "You ain't got no say. You're headed straight for a hangman's noose, anyhow."

Tilton spoke for the first time. "Take a vote, Scobey."

"You want to give him up?"

"I sure as hell do."

Owen said, "Quade?"

"You know how I vote. No."

"Kate?"

"We can't give him up. Not to them."

"Matt?"

"No, Owen," Matt didn't look at Tilton but kept his glance steadily on his feet.

Owen said, "You two are voted down. So keep your mouth shut about it after this."

Neither Tilton nor Smith replied. Owen asked, "Quade you think they'll come again tonight?"

"Huh uh. Take a look."

Owen glanced down toward the plain. A tiny fire was winking there, a fire that grew rapidly even as he watched. Quade said, "They're settin' up camp for the night. But they'll be back at dawn."

"Then we'd just as well eat. And I'll get something to fix his leg." He headed toward the rear of the wagon. Smith crawled under it, as though to sleep.

The shot was almost deafening this close. Owen whirled, snatching out his gun.

But no Indian had fired that gun. It had discharged beneath the wagon not half a dozen feet from where Owen stood.

He knew instantly what it was. He took three quick steps, stooped and seized Smith's feet. He dragged him out. Infuriated, he kicked savagely.

Smith grunted and doubled. Owen shoved his gun into its holster and kicked again, almost frenziedly. He was filled with revulsion, the way he'd always felt killing a rattlesnake.

He heard Quade's voice. "No use doin' that. Chavez is dead."

Owen stopped. He stood there glaring furiously down at Smith's dimly seen, doubled form on the ground.

"You won't get a chance to hang for that other killin' now. You'll hang for this one in Abilene!"

Smith was shaking violently, as he got to his feet. At first, Owen thought it was fear, then he realized the man was laughing—almost hysterically. Owen clenched his fists. He strode angrily away into the darkness, knowing that if he stayed, he would kill the man.

Not that he'd been so fond of Chavez. But a man doesn't live that way—killing his fellow men whenever it becomes expedient. That was an animal's way.

He stayed away for almost half an hour, walking in the silent night, letting his temper cool itself. Then he went back, calling out while he was still a hundred feet away.

Chavez had been dragged away into the darkness. Smith and Quade and Tilton were beneath the wagon. Matt and Kate sat together near the wagon tongue.

Kate said, "There are some cold biscuits here."

Owen took several and forced himself to eat. He drank a little water to wash them down. Kate asked fearfully, "What are we going to do now?"

He said, "I'll take Chavez to their camp as long as he's already dead. Then we'll wait and see."

"Do you think it will do any good?"

"Might. I don't know. They've lost a lot of men. Maybe with Chavez dead, they won't think it's worth it any more."

He walked around the wagon and untied his horse. He said, "Quade."

The man came crawling out from beneath the wagon. Owen said, "Help me load him. Where is he?"

"Over here. You goin' to haul him down to 'em?"

"Uh huh. They can't hurt him now."

Quade led the way into the darkness and Owen followed. Between them, they lifted Chavez to the saddle. The horse fidgeted worriedly, but Owen held him still, then mounted while Quade steadied the inert burden. From his saddle. Owen said softly, "If I don't make it back, I want you to do something for me."

"Sure, Scobey."

"Kill that goddam Smith. Then try and make it to Abilene with Kate and Matt. Forget the cattle. Just get away."

"All right. I can do that, all right."

"No even breaks for Smith. Kill him like you would a wolf."

"All right."

Owen swung his horse around and headed down the hill.

He had made it sound simple, delivering this body to the Indians' camp. He had purposely made it sound that way. But it wasn't simple. It wasn't simple at all.

In spite of the fire burning so openly down there, he knew the Indians were on guard. They were certainly aware that they might be attacked during the night.

He rode slowly, therefore, letting his horse pick its own way down the slope. Even so, he made more noise than he could afford.

At the bottom, he swung right, down wind. If he approached the camp from that direction, he would eliminate the chance that the Indians' horses would smell his own horse and give him away.

He paralleled the arroyo for a quarter mile before he looked for a crossing. Shortly thereafter, he found one and rode his horse down into it and out on the other side.

As he approached the Indian camp, the tension in him began to increase. He held his reins in his left hand, steadied Chavez' body with his knees, and held his revolver in his right.

The minutes dragged. Everything in him screamed for haste, but he continued to let the horse pick its own slow way along.

He could see the fire plainly now. He could see

the lumped shapes of Indians sleeping near it on the ground. He could see two, walking slowly back and forth with rifles in their hands. He knew that others were standing guard out here in the darkness away from the fire's light. They would see him before he could possibly see them.

Alertly, tensely, he rode along. The distance between himself and the fire dwindled to three hundred yards, two hundred, a hundred. And no shots racketed in the silent night. No shouts rang out.

Fifty yards. He heard a flurry of movement on his right and his spurs dug spasmodically into his horse's sides. The startled animal leaped ahead.

A rifle muzzle flashed from the direction of the sound. The bullet must have passed close behind him, for he heard the angry sound it made. Then his horse was running and Owen's spurs were raking him mercilessly as he did.

He was in the center of the Indian camp so quickly that he scarcely had time to ready himself. He slid himself back in the saddle and put a foot beneath Chavez' body on the right side. Raising the foot with all the strength in his leg, he heaved the body across the saddle.

His horse shied as he did and the body slid clear and thumped on the ground, rolled limply and came to a stop. Then Owen was beyond the circle of firelight and thundering wildly through the inky dark.

There were guttural Indian shouts behind. There were a few ragged shots and the sharp twang of a bowstring, twice. Then he was clear and his horse was running free.

He swung left toward the arroyo. He found the crossing by following the pounded trail of the cattle entering it, visible even at night as a lighter streak upon the plain. He plunged out of the arroyo and headed up the slope.

There was nothing to do now but wait for dawn. He wouldn't know if delivering Chavez' body to them had done any good until then. Quite possibly, it had not. The Indians might well feel cheated because the man was dead and continue their attack. Or they might now want to avenge the death of their companions, killed in the skirmish at dusk.

But he had done everything he could. All any of them could do now was wait, and hope.

None of them got any sleep, though most of them tried. The men sat in a little group before the wagon, watching the Indian camp a mile away on the plain. They were too far away to see what was going on, but it wasn't hard to guess. They were mutilating Chavez, even though he was dead.

Kate and Matt sat huddled together, their backs against the wagon tongue. Owen paced nervously back and forth.

Near midnight, the fire down on the plain dwindled and went completely out. A chill came across the land and the stars seemed to grow brighter than they had been before. Somewhere a coyote barked, to be answered by another, farther away.

Owen sat down next to Kate. She had an arm around Matt and was holding him close to her, against the cold but against the fear of dawn as well. Her voice was soft and small. "Do you think—"

"There's a good chance they'll go away. Chavez was the one they wanted. They know another attack will be as costly as the last."

"And if they don't?"

"Then we'll make it as expensive as we can."

Even more softly than before, she said, "I'm sorry I got you into this. It wasn't fair."

Owen asked, "Is Matt asleep?"

"I don't know. I think he is."

Owen said guardedly, "I'm not sorry, Kate. If you'd gone to Fort Worth—" He felt a sudden nervousness. "Damn it, I don't know what's going to happen tomorrow. I just want you to know—Kate, will you marry me when we get to Abilene?"

She was silent for a long long time. His nervousness increased until it was almost intolerable. And her voice, when it came, was so soft he could scarcely hear. "Yes, Owen. Yes."

Hell of a place to propose, he thought. Hell of a time, too. He turned and took her face between his calloused hands. He thought her cheeks were wet. He kissed her on the mouth and found it soft, and innocent, and sweet.

The ache touched his chest, the ache of need for her, but it was pleasant tonight because it was no longer a hopeless thing. She said in a voice both determined and very frightened, "Owen, we could slip away. I think Matt is asleep. We don't know—about tomorrow. I want you to hold me close. I—" She stopped, caught up in her own confusion.

Owen's blood raced. His heart thumped almost audibly in his chest. She withdrew her arm from Matt and he stirred and spoke, though his words were indistinguishable.

A voice came softly from beyond the wagon, Quade's voice. "It's gettin' light."

Owen said, "Damn!" Time must have passed faster than he thought. He kissed her again, this time urgently. When he drew away, she said breathlessly, "Owen, we have all our life. . . ."

He pushed himself to his feet. He could see

Quade standing in a cleared area beyond the wagon. He glanced down at Kate, able to see her features dimly in the growing, grayish light. There were tears on her cheeks, but her mouth was smiling. He switched his glance to Matt and found the boy watching him steadily and expressionlessly. There was nothing in that look and its very emptiness was indicative of sulleness and anger. "Why, the kid's jealous." Owen thought.

He walked to where Quade stood and peered intently in the direction of the Indian camp. It was still too dark to see anything clearly at more than a hundred yards.

Anxiously they waited, joined a few moments later by Tilton and Smith and Matt. Kate stayed at the wagon, watching them.

Slowly the light grew stronger. Slowly the range of their vision increased.

But not until they could see half a mile beyond the place where the Indian camp had been did Owen's lungs draw deeply of the morning air. The Indian camp was gone. Nothing remained to show that it had ever been there—nothing but a lumped shape that last night had been Chavez.

☆ 17 ☆

MOST of this day was spent in rounding up the scattered herd, in gathering the horses, which had scattered, too, but had not gone as far. In early afternoon, the herd trailed north again.

And the tension between the men, slackened by common danger the day before, renewed itself. Tilton stared across the rising dust at Owen often during the day and while his expression was unreadable because of the distance and the dust, Owen knew it was smoldering with anger and with hate. He doubted if Tilton had ever been beaten before with fists alone. Tilton preferred to use his gun, with which he was unbeatable. To be pounded insensible, particularly in front of Matt, whom he wanted to impress . . .

In camp that night, Quade continued to taunt the man, slyly and carefully going to but not beyond the point where Tilton's self-control would slip. And Smith, rested by the halt several days before, watched Kate more intently than he ever had.

Perhaps it was the change in Kate herself rather than Smith's being more rested. For there was a change. Her face was more relaxed and somehow softer, too. Her mouth smiled often when Owen was around. She went out of her way to do little things for him.

Owen watched them all, watched Tilton when he was with Matt and often as not horned in. He watched Smith whenever he was in camp. He watched Quade and listened in on Quade's taunting whenever possible, alert to prevent an explosion if Quade should go too far.

Kate drove the wagon all the time. She had no choice because Quade was riding point.

This way, the days dragged and the miles fell slowly behind. They crossed the Cimarron and turned northeast, heading for Abilene.

The third day after crossing the Cimarron, they struck a cattle trail pounded into the plain only days before. And the next morning, it was Tilton who was gone.

Infuriated, suspecting where Tilton had gone and why, Owen put Matt on the right flank of the herd and himself rode both flank and drag positions. He changed horses ten times that first day, as often on the second and the third. The old exhaustion he'd thought himself toughened against returned.

And at night, out riding the perimeter of the herd, he did something he hadn't done for years. He practiced with his gun, practiced getting it out of its holster fast, thumbing back the hammer and snapping it at an imaginary target, knowing even as he did that it would do him little good.

If Matt asked him once, he asked him a dozen times, "Where do you reckon Mr. Tilton went? You think anything could have happened to him? You think he'll be coming back?"

And Owen would reply sourly, forcing into his voice a patience he did not feel, "He'll be back, Matt. You can count on that." To himself, he would think bitterly, "He'll be back when he's got his arrangements made."

So when he saw Tilton riding toward them from the distance on the morning of the fourth day, he was not surprised.

Tilton avoided Matt, who was on the right flank of the herd and closest to him. Instead, he circled the drag and approached Owen immediately. There was still smoldering hatred in his eyes but it was tempered now by triumph he couldn't quite conceal.

Owen said, "I take it you've made your deal."

Tilton's eyes flashed. "I've made it."

"All right. Don't beat around the bush. Come out with it." Tilton said, "We stay on this trail tomorrow. Then we turn 'em east."

"How you going to explain that to Quade and Smith? They've got a cut coming, too, you know."

"How you explain it to them is your concern. But you'd better make it good."

"What happens when we turn east?"

"You won't need to worry about that end of it, Scobey. It'll be taken care of when the right time comes."

"And Miss Pryor? What does she get out of it?"

Tilton grinned unpleasantly at him. "Depends on how you handle your end. On whether you try anything stupid or not. Maybe she'll get ten per cent. Maybe she won't get a God-damned thing."

Owen scowled and said softly, "The horse is broke to ride. But don't try the spurs just yet."

"Why not, Scobey? What'll you do? Tell the boy yourself? Like hell you will. You know damned well if he finds out, he'll walk out on you. He'll go with me and I'll take him, too. Not because I want the little bastard but because I know what I can do with him. I'll make a bad one out of him, Scobey. He'll hang before he's twenty-five."

Owen's hands clenched tight as they rested on his saddle horn. Abruptly he whirled his horse and pounded back to the drag, where he spent a good half hour rounding up stragglers at a hard gallop and pushing them on to join the herd.

His face stayed set in a twisted, infuriated mask. He was being asked to betray not only Kate and Matt, but Quade and Smith as well. Tilton, the whip in his hand, was showing characteristic greed. He was going to take it all.

Nor was betrayal all that was involved. By turning the herd east, by putting the others at the mercy of a gang of border toughs with whom Tilton had undoubtedly made his deal, he was risking their lives as well. A life meant nothing to the border gangs, even if it was a boy's or a woman's life. War had hardened them to murder. Killing a few drovers, a woman and a boy wouldn't bother them in the least.

Tilton circled the herd and relieved Matt. They talked for several minutes while Matt glanced often and nervously toward Owen across the rising dust of the moving herd. At last, he pulled back, but with obvious reluctance, and again assumed his position in the drag of the herd.

Tormented with indecision, Owen watched him working the drag as efficiently as a man. He imagined the look that would be on Matt's face when Tilton told him the truth, when Tilton told him Owen had been the lawman he had taught Matt to despise.

There was pain in that. There was pain in thinking of his life without the boy. But the pain was worse when he thought of what Tilton could do with the embittered youngster.

Teach him to use a gun. Teach him contempt for law and for human life. Teach him distrust and greed. Point him down the path that could lead only to a scaffold and a hangman's noose.

Was a herd of cattle worth this? He was going to marry Kate. He would give her a home and protection in the land she loved and in which she wanted to remain. Her purpose in bringing the cattle north would be served even if she lost the cattle themselves.

They could go back home, the three of them. Next year, they could gather another herd and bring it north.

Yet even as he argued thus, he knew that he was wrong. Giving Tilton the herd would not only be a betrayal, it would serve no purpose, either, in the long run. Having made blackmail pay off so handsomely once, Tilton wouldn't give it up. He'd be riding Owen's back as long as Owen had anything he wanted. Which meant that next year, with the next herd, too, he would appear before the herd reached Abilene. He'd take that herd as he had taken this.

"I can tell Matt myself before next year," Owen argued. But the argument didn't convince him. Because he'd have two things to explain—the death of Matt's father and the betrayal of Kate and the men.

He rode out the day on the flank of the herd. The work helped, but it didn't help enough.

He was moody and preoccupied that night in camp. Tilton watched him, a faintly mocking quality mingling with the dislike in his eyes. Matt seemed puzzled, both by Tilton's disappearance and by Owen's preoccupation.

But Quade didn't let up. Eating, he stared across the fire at Tilton. "Kill anyone while you were gone?" he asked, and when Tilton scowled at him, said apologetically, "No call to get riled. I'm just keepin' score for you."

There was an edge in his voice, an edge that betrayed his knowledge that they were very close to Abilene and to the end of the drive.

This might be an out, Owen thought. Let Quade taunt Tilton beyond endurance. When Tilton took it up, interfere and . . .

The thought was intolerable. However he excused that course, however he might tell himself it was justified by necessity, he knew it would still be murder. There were really only two courses open to him. One was to turn the herd east as Tilton had demanded. The other was to pick a quarrel with Tilton and shoot it out with him. Which would accomplish nothing useful. Tilton still would get the herd because Owen would be dead. He would leave Kate and Matt stranded in Abilene. Owen couldn't hope to match Tilton's blinding speed with a gun.

Tilton glowered at Quade. "What the hell's your beef, old man? What have I ever done to you? I never saw you in my life until I joined up with Richards' troop."

"I ain't famous like you."

"No, but you'll be dead if you don't shut up. I never shot a man in the back in my life. I never shot an unarmed man. If you've been keeping score as good as you say you have, you know it, too. But that don't mean I won't."

Owen's puzzlement increased. Quade must be succeeding with his taunts. Tilton was actually troubling to explain himself, to try and justify himself.

Quade persisted, "Where was you durin' the war, Mr. Tilton? That's a part of your life I ain't quite got straight."

Tilton opened his mouth, then clamped it tightly shut. He growled, "To hell with you! If you know so much—"

"Well, I know a little bit. You was on our side, all right, if you want to call that the Southern side."

Tilton scowled into the fire, refusing to look up.

Quade mused, "Missouri Bushrangers, they called 'em. They was just right for you, wasn't they? There was money in ridin' with them—plunder in every town they burned."

"You mouthy old bastard!" Tilton rose to his feet threateningly.

Quade said hastily, "No offense, man. No offense."

"Damn you!"

Owen said sharply, "Tilton!"

Owen's voice quieted the man instantly. He could almost see Tilton's mind yank itself from its preoccupation with Quade and force itself to dwell upon the prospective profit in the theft of the cattle herd.

Owen turned his head to scowl at Quade. "And you let up, too. I don't know what's in your craw and I don't give a damn. But let up on him until we get to Abilene."

Until we get to Abilene. An irony, that. They weren't going to Abilene.

He strode angrily away from the fire. Kate spoke to him from where she was standing near the wagon. "Owen . . ."

He only scowled at her. Matt stared after him as he left the circle of firelight, puzzlement lingering in his eyes. Furiously Owen strode across the darkened plain, fighting a battle with which no one could give him help.

He walked for a mile or more, then turned and

more slowly retraced his steps. There was really only one decision he could make. There had never been more than one. But until the time for decisions came, he'd keep it to himself.

☆ 18 ☆

HE was sorry he'd glared at Kate. He thought that perhaps he should share his problem with her but decided immediately against it. He knew what her reaction would be. She would want to give Tilton the herd. Or, at least, he thought she would.

A strange uneasiness suddenly crowded these thoughts from his mind. He began to hurry back toward camp.

Oddly, instead of diminishing, the uneasiness increased. And Owen increased his pace until he was almost running.

What could have gone wrong? Was it only the state of his mind causing the feeling? Was it only his knowledge of all the cross currents of hostility within the camp and his fear that one or more of them would leap out of control?

He had heard no shots, so it probably was not Tilton and Quade. Smith, then. Smith. . . .

He increased the speed of his lunging run, panting softly now. God, he shouldn't have come so far. He hadn't realized . . .

But Kate wouldn't have left the camp. She was afraid of Smith. Unless she had followed him . . . He remembered the things that had been in her

149

face as he stalked out of camp. Hurt. Puzzlement. But compassion, too.

She might have been worried enough about him to forget her own fears. She might have come after him. And Smith . . .

His breath now came rapidly as he plunged across the uneven, grassy plain. His ears were tuned for sound.

He heard something and hauled up in an abrupt halt. The sound was not repeated, but he thought he knew what it had been—a cry, muffled by a hand perhaps—a cry that would be heard no better in camp than it was out here.

But where? Oh, God, where? Reason told him to stop until the sound was repeated, until he could place the exact location of it. Urgency would not let him. His thoughts dwelt unwillingly on the terror behind that sound, on the things that were happening to her to cause it.

He ran until he was almost exhausted. Then he stopped again. His breath came rapidly and harshly as his starving lungs fought for air.

He tried to quiet the sound of his breathing so that he could hear. He stood utterly motionless, fury growing uncontrollably in him. Smith. He'd kill the man the way he'd kill a tarantula or a scorpion. With revulsion and relief. With fierce pleasure.

The sound again—slight and so faintly heard as to seem imagined. From over on his left it came and he lunged into motion as soon as it reached his ears.

Not far—a hundred yards, perhaps—and his eyes picked movement out of the almost complete blackness of the plain.

He shouted, "Kate!" and swerved toward that movement he had seen. A sickness was in him now.

Had he come too late? Was she lying hurt and ravished on the ground, beaten and—

He plunged on and from ten feet away saw Smith struggle to his feet and try to escape.

The man went less than half a dozen feet. Then Owen was on him, striking him with his body and knocking him sprawling far more than a dozen feet.

He clawed on, the hurt sound of Kate's weeping driving him, turning his fury into a berserk desire to maim and kill, to inflict pain equal to that Kate was suffering.

Why had he been fool enough to let Smith remain at all? Why hadn't he killed him or driven him away when Richards first told him what Smith was?

He reached Smith and grappled for his throat. Smith raised a knee into his groin, fighting now as if he knew he was fighting for his life.

Owen's mind refused to notice the pain, which was like a knife ripping into his abdominal wall. His hands closed on Smith's throat and bit deep into it, forcing the windpipe closed, bruising with their almost maniacal strength.

Smith's arms came around his own, the hands clawing, groping until they found Owen's face. Then the thumbs went with vicious and practiced precision into the sockets of his eyes.

Only the excruciating pain, only the knowledge that in seconds he would be blinded, released the grip of Owen's hands. Loose, he yanked back his head, felt relief from that terrible pain, and smashed Smith's face with his hard-knuckled, fisted hands.

Smith struggled like a bucking horse, thrashing back and forth beneath him, and at last flung him off and came free. Rising, he managed to reach his gun and snatch it from its holster. He fired, almost in Owen's face.

Powder burns seared Owen's skin and the flash blinded him. He plunged forward, groping, and managed to seize Smith's arm.

Wrist in left hand, elbow in right, as though he were snapping a stick of firewood, he brought that arm down across his rising knee.

He was still blind, perhaps partly from Smith's gouging thumbs, partly from the muzzle flash so close to his eyes. But he didn't need to see right now. He heard with fierce and gloating satisfaction the dull, snapping sound of the arm bone as it broke. He heard the shrill, high, almost womanish scream of pain that tore from Smith's panting lips.

He hung onto the wrist, released the elbow, stepped back and yanked. The scream died as suddenly as though a hand had been clamped over the deserter's mouth. His body went limp as that of a doll and he came stumbling against Owen, nearly taking his legs out from under him. He lay at Owen's feet, alive but without consciousness, and Owen yelled furiously, "No, by God! No! You don't get out of it that easy!" He kicked brutally and his heel smashed squarely into the unconscious Smith's face.

Hands pulled at him and Kate's voice screamed, "No, Owen! No! I'm all right!"

He stopped his boot in midflight. He whirled and seized her with fierce tenderness in his arms. "All right? How could you be? It was so damn long. . . ."

"I fought him, Owen. I fought—" Her restraint suddenly broke all bounds and wild hysteria tore at her like a hurricane wind whipping through the branches of a tree.

He heard the sound of a horse's hoofs and Quade hauled his plunging horse to a halt a dozen feet away. Owen yelled, "Throw me your rope. The loop."

The loop came down. Owen pulled himself away from Kate, stooped and put the loop on Smith's two feet. He yanked it tight. "Dally the end and go on back to camp."

The rope pulled tight. He heard Quade's voice. "Smith?"

"Yeah. Where's Tilton? And Matt?"

"With the herd on the other side of camp. They relieved Smith to eat."

"And where were you?"

"Checkin' the horses. That's why I wasn't—"

Owen said, "Never mind. Take him in to camp." He watched unfeelingly as Quade rode his horse slowly toward camp with Smith skidding feet first behind him on the end of his rope.

He returned to Kate, whose hysterics had subsided but whose body still shook as though with a violent chill.

His anger had quieted. He could feel pity now and concern deeper than he had ever felt before. He said softly, "I'm sorry. I should have killed him or driven him out of camp. I knew what he was. I knew what the danger was."

"I'm all right, Owen." There was a softly insistent intensity about her voice. "I'm bruised and skinned and my clothes are torn, but nothing else. You're not to kill him."

He had never loved her more than he did right now. He grinned a little to himself in the darkness, with weak relief, thinking how surprised Smith must have been. Kate was strong for a woman. Smith must have thought he'd tangled with a tiger. He said, "Come on."

She walked along with him, limping a little, and

Owen took his time, holding her arm so that she would not wrench her already hurt leg. Just before they reached the fire, she stopped. "Tilton is threatening you, isn't he?"

"Yes."

"Do you want to tell me why?"

"No."

She was silent for several long moments. He stared gloomily toward the fire, watched Quade dismount and take his loop off the unconscious Smith.

"There is only one thing he could want from you. Give it to him, Owen. Give him the whole herd if that is what he wants."

It was a moment before Owen could speak. She had just undergone one of the most terrible experiences of her life, second only to the raid in which her parents were killed. Yet already she was thinking of him, worrying about him, wanting to help if she could. He said hoarsely, "Thank you, Kate."

She gazed up into his face for a long moment. Her own face was smudged with dust and there was a skinned place on her nose, another on her cheek. Her mouth was puffy and bleeding slightly. But her eyes were soft as she stood on tiptoe and kissed him lightly on the mouth. Then she turned and limped to the wagon to change her torn and dirty clothes.

Owen stalked to the firelight. He looked down at the unconscious Smith on the ground. He stared at Quade, waiting across the fire. "Get his horse."

Quade disappeared obediently and silently into the darkness. He came back a few moments later, leading Smith's horse.

Owen said, "Over here."

Quade led the horse to him. Owen stooped, picked Smith up and slung him roughly across the saddle, belly down. He hooked Smith's belt over the saddle horn. He tied the horse's reins up.

He left the animal standing there, went to the wagon and got the whip. Returning, he slashed Smith's horse savagely across the rump, yelling suddenly and shrilly as he did.

The animal lunged away, galloping hard before he disappeared out of the fire's light. Owen heard the pound of his hoofs slowly diminish and die away.

He felt weak, drained of his strength. He stared moodily into the fire. Smith would probably die. His arm was broken and it wasn't even certain he could free himself from the saddle horn.

Owen discovered that he didn't even care. He felt too numb.

Chavez and Smith were gone now. There remained only Tilton and Quade, Kate and Matt and himself. Not enough. But then, they had never really had enough men to handle the herd properly. They'd just have to go on and hope that no emergencies arose.

The horse herd was rope-coralled less than a quarter mile from camp. The cattle were quiet and the sky was clear. They would have to leave the wagon behind tomorrow. Matt could drive the horse herd. Quade could ride point. Kate would have to bring up the drag.

She came from the wagon, still limping, wearing clean clothes—some of Owen's—as baggy as the others had been. She had washed her face and combed her hair. There was still considerable shock in her eyes and strain evident on her face but she was smiling now.

She came to where he stood beside the fire. She stopped beside him and gazed steadily into the flames. She said, "I meant what I said, Owen. Give Tilton the cattle. You and I and Matt can go on to Abilene. When we're rested, we can go home."

Owen shook his head. "If he gets away with it once, he'll try again. Do you think we could ever bring a herd north again if we gave this one to him?"

"It has to do with Matt, doesn't it? Next year, Matt will be older. Whatever Tilton threatens to tell him—well, in a year, he'll be able to understand."

Owen shook his head again. "In five years, maybe. Not in one."

"Then we'll wait five years."

He didn't reply, but there was something tight in his throat.

Suddenly and harshly, he said, "I killed Matt's father. Tilton saw it. I was the deputy in that story of Tilton's. I murdered Matt's father when he wasn't even reaching for his gun."

"That isn't true. That can't be true."

His face twisted. "The hell of it is I don't know whether it's true or not. I've gone over it a thousand times in my mind. I've dreamed about it a thousand nights and I still don't know."

"But you must have thought—"

He nodded bitterly. "Yes. I thought he was reaching for his gun. The way he turned, there was nothing else I could think. But I never actually saw the gun. He died with it still in its holster."

It was Kate who was silent now, and Owen felt a compulsion to make her understand, or a compulsion to make himself understand, to make his own mind stop condemning him.

He said, "I didn't even try for a killing shot. I tried to hit him in the arm. But he was turning too fast. He moved right into the path of the bullet."

"Is it guilt that makes you keep Matt?"

He turned and scowled at her. "Do you think it's guilt?" He was suddenly angry with her because she had put into words a question that had troubled him more than once. Then the scowl faded. He said wearily, honestly, "It was guilt at first, I guess. But it isn't now." He realized for the first time that that was exactly true. It may have been guilt at first but it wasn't any more.

Kate's voice was small and firm. "You have only two choices, Owen. Tell Matt yourself or give Tilton the herd."

Owen nodded.

"And you have only tomorrow to decide."

He nodded again.

"Don't worry, Owen. Whatever you decide will be right. And it will be all right with me." She put her hands on his arms and turned him until he was facing her. Her eyes were soft and warm. "It wasn't murder, Owen. Not unless you've changed an awful lot since then."

He forced himself to smile. "Thanks, Kate. I needed someone to tell me that."

Kate had said there were only two choices he could make. But there was a third. He swung to his horse and rode away in the direction of the herd to take Matt's place on guard.

☆ 19 ☆

THE next day was a nightmare. In early morning, the horse herd got away from Matt and galloped several miles before Owen could catch up and turn them back. Returning, he found the cattle stopped.

It took nearly an hour of hard riding to get them moving again, but they seemed to know there were not enough men to keep them moving north. All day, bunches of them strayed away and had to be returned. And while this was being done, the main herd would slow and stop. The miracle was that they moved at all.

Owen briefly considered riding north to Abilene and hiring more men. He discarded the idea immediately. By the time he could get there and return, there wouldn't be any herd to drive. Tilton would see to that. He could get the men with whom he had made his deal faster than Owen could ride in, hire a crew and return.

He saw little of Tilton that day, little of Kate and nothing at all of Matt. He saw little but dust, and cattle, and glaring sun.

He stood first watch that night with the herd, went in at midnight and stirred Tilton with his toe. The man got up, stumbled to his horse and rode out. Owen lay down and shook his blanket over him.

Tired as he was, it was a while before he went to sleep. He kept thinking about tomorrow.

He dreaded it because no matter what he decided, he was going to be wrong. Giving the cattle to Tilton would buy him a year but no more than that. Refusing to give him the cattle would cost him not only Matt's respect, but the boy himself. A shoot-out with Tilton could end only one way—with Owen dead. To kill Tilton any way but face to face not only was foreign to his nature but would prove, to Matt and to himself, that he was exactly what Tilton claimed he was.

He slept at last, but woke in the first gray light of dawn. Over the fire, as they ate the last of the slim rations Kate had packed behind her saddle yesterday and drank coffee brewed from the water in their canteens, Tilton stared at him watchfully, apparently trying to guess what his decision was going to be.

Finished, they killed the fire and mounted up.

"Now," thought Owen and glanced at Quade. He said, "Take 'em to Abilene."

Quade stared at him peculiarly, plainly wondering why he should use that particular phrase now after so many weeks on the trail. But Owen didn't see. His eyes rested steadily on Tilton's face.

The man froze for an instant, then met Owen's glance with his own. A certain watchfulness was in his eyes, a certain brightness that had not been there before.

Matt was already riding out, heading for the horse herd, rope-corralled a quarter mile away.

The faintest of shrugs touched Tilton's shoulders. His mouth became a thin, hard, angry line. His eyes narrowed to slits. "You'd better change your mind. I'll get 'em anyway."

Owen said implacably, "Abilene."

"Suit yourself. It's your funeral."

"Or yours."

"Want to try it now?"

Owen was momentarily silent. Kate interjected sharply, "Mr. Quade, we're heading east. We're not going to Abilene."

Quade frowned. "East! North! What the hell's goin' on? What's everybody talkin' about?"

Owen said evenly, "Nothing. "Were going to Abilene. Get started, Quade."

Tilton reined his horse in the direction Matt had gone, turning his head as he did, so that he could keep his steady glance on Owen. He yelled, "Matt! Wait a minute. There's something I want to talk to you about."

Owen swung his horse slowly so that his right side remained toward the gunman. His voice was suddenly like the crack of a whip. "Hold it, Tilton!"

That instant was an eternity. Tilton's hands hauled in on his reins so that his horse would not be moving when he shot. The horse pulled up, but still Tilton waited and Owen knew the man wanted the horse completely still.

The imminence of death was like a coldness in Owen's body. His hand, hanging so close to the grip of his gun, felt clammy and cold. He would never match Tilton's speed. But at this range—at more than thirty yards—there was a good chance Tilton's first shot would miss, or at least miss a vital spot. Which would give Owen the chance he had to have.

What was happening had the quality of a nightmare in Owen's mind. Quade sat his horse, frozen, fifteen feet away. Kate was moving, trying to get her horse into the line of fire, thinking perhaps that this would prevent the inevitable from happening.

Off toward the horse herd, Matt had stopped, and turned, but had not yet started to ride back.

Kate was only a dozen feet from her objective. Only a few seconds remained. More tense than he had ever been in his life before, Owen's mind willed his hand to seize the grip of his gun.

The shot came with deafening suddenness, totally unexpected and not immediately understood by any of the five.

Tensed as he was, there was only one thing Owen Scobey could do. He felt the cold, hard walnut grips of his gun and felt the gun come clear.

He couldn't understand why he hadn't been hit; he couldn't understand why no powder smoke hung in the air near where Tilton was.

Tilton's gun was in his hand, just now coming up. Slower than Owen's gun. Slower . . .

Another shot bellowed out—and not from Tilton's gun, or Owen's, either. It came from the right, from behind, from more than fifty yards away. Now Owen understood why it had puzzled him before. It wasn't a revolver shot. It was from a rifle, louder, deeper, more menacing.

He felt his horse jerk spasmodically with the impact of the bullet. He realized the horse was falling beneath him in time to leap from the saddle and roll clear. Thrashing and kicking, the horse fell.

Owen still held his revolver but he hadn't a chance to use it now. Tilton's gun snapped around, its muzzle following him with unerring speed as he rolled to a stop on the ground.

In seconds, he would see smoke billow from that gaping bore. Or would he? Might not the bullet snuff out his life so quickly that he wouldn't even see the smoke?

He tried desperately to bring the gun to bear, still vaguely puzzled as to the source of that rifle shot.

And then he heard a shout, one that froze Tilton as effectively as a bullet might have done. "Tilton! God damn you, you're mine, not his! I've been waitin' for this for years!"

Owen came to his knees, his gun ready now. He saw Quade standing spread-legged on the ground, his rifle in his hands and pointed straight at Tilton's chest.

There was no time to consider how complicated the situation had become. Owen stood rigid, stunned, momentarily unable to move.

Quade's voice rose, quavering, as emotion got its grip on him. "I want you to know why I'm killin' you before I do it! No! Don't turn! My son was number nine on your rotten list. But there won't be any more. This is the end of the track for you!"

Tilton's glance shifted like lightning from Quade to Owen. There was something in his eyes Owen had never seen there before. Panic perhaps, still controlled. And fear. And doubt in himself.

Tilton made his decision. His gun, which had pointed at neither Owen nor Quade, swung toward Owen with the hammer back.

It came around like a whip and fired as it came in line. Owen's shot came almost simultaneously, blending like an echo with the report of Tilton's gun.

Tilton jerked with the impact of the bullet but did not fall from his saddle. His horse reared, its body momentarily coming between the two opponents.

Owen felt a blow to his thigh that was like the kick of a mule. His stunned mind thought, "I'm hit," but he was so preoccupied following Tilton's form with the muzzle of his gun that he hadn't time to think of it.

The report of Quade's big bore rifle made puny the echoes of Tilton's and Owen's shots. And the bullet struck Tilton squarely in the chest.

The sound was sodden and dull, yet there was a slapping quality to it. Almost overshadowed by the monstrous roar of the rifle, it nevertheless was plain and unmistakable in Owen's ears.

Tilton was driven from the saddle as though struck by a cannon ball.

He sprawled awkwardly in midair for an instant, then struck the ground, limp and completely still. There was a hole in the middle of his back, torn and red and big enough for Owen to have put a fist in it.

The rifle roared again from fifty yards away. This bullet torn into the still body of Owen's horse with a sound very similar to that of Quade's bullet striking the gunman's chest.

Owen yelled. "Smith! It must be Smith!"

"Cover me!"

Owen crawled to the body of his horse, raised up and fired three quick shots in the direction of a blue cloud of powder smoke hanging motionless in the air. His gun snapped on an empty and he yanked his rifle from the saddle boot and fired again.

Quade was halfway there, bending low, sprinting with speed and agility surprising in a man his age. Not directly toward Smith's hiding place but a little to the left of it.

Owen saw something move behind the smoke and fired instantly. It disappeared. Quade reached the point toward which he was heading and flopped to the ground.

Owen couldn't see him now for he lay in a slight

hollow. He watched not the spot where Quade had disappeared but that slowly dissipating cloud of bluish powder smoke.

Quade stood up and yelled, "All right! He's dead!"

Owen got to his feet. He walked toward the spot where Smith had been. The man lay on his back, staring up at the sky with open, sightless eyes. There was a small, bluish hole in his forehead over one of his eyes. Beneath his head was a spreading pool of blood.

"You got him when he raised up. He was already dead when he hit the ground."

Owen turned and walked back toward Kate. The fight seemed to have been going on for hours but he realized suddenly that it couldn't have lasted much more than a minute. Matt, who had been less than three hundred yards away, was just now arriving at the scene.

The boy's face was white with shock. He stared at Owen with eyes that seemed to beg for reassurance and support.

Kate also was looking at Owen, but with a different expression in her eyes, one he had seen there before. Confidence. Trust. And compassion, too, because she understood, the terrible strain that had just been released in him.

He felt as if he was drained of strength. He thought his face must look as white and bloodless as it felt. His knees were weak and if he tried to stand still, he could feel the tremors in them.

Quade had followed him back and now stood looking down at Tilton. He seemed older than he had been ten minutes ago. Whatever it was that had kept him going so long was gone. He glanced at Owen, his face almost gray. "I don't feel what I thought I'd feel," he said. "There was no more satisfaction in that than there is in a mirage. He killed my boy. The kid was only nineteen and cocky. Tilton didn't have to take him on, but he did. It was murder. But because my kid drew his gun, they called it self-defense. Self-defense, hell!" He scowled confusedly. "I been after Tilton for fifteen years, off and on. Now it's like—" He didn't finish. He stood looking down at Tilton with a vacant face and vacant eyes.

☆ 20 ☆

OWEN glanced from Quade to Kate and then to Matt. Nothing had been solved for him, he realized now. Tilton's death didn't solve a thing. The secret he had tried so long to hide still stood like a wall between Matt and himself.

He took a step toward Matt and almost fell as his wounded leg gave away. He recovered and stood with his weight on the good leg. He could feel the warmth of blood now and glanced down.

His pants leg was soaked with blood. Kate said worriedly, "You sit down. Let me fix that leg."

He went over and sat down on the rump of his dead horse. With his knife, he carefully slit the leg of his pants immediately over the wound.

Kate rummaged in her saddlebags until she found some clean cloth. She laid a compress over the bleeding wound, then tied it up. It wasn't a bad wound but it was bleedingly freely, and painful now.

Matt had dismounted. Now, suddenly, he ran away from the others. He stopped fifty yards away and Owen heard him retching violently.

Owen got up and headed toward Matt, hobbling on the wounded leg, which pained him more with

166

every step. Behind him, he heard Quade say sharply, "Wait a minute, Scobey!"

He stopped, turned. Quade was pointing toward the south. Dust hung in the air back there and a group of a dozen men was riding toward them.

Tilton's men? Owen didn't know. If it was Tilton's men, they were finished. Four of them couldn't fight off twelve even if all four of them had been in condition to fight.

He walked out toward the group and waited. The riders drew near, halted while they were yet thirty feet away.

They didn't look like border toughs. They looked like drovers.

One of them, older than the rest, asked, "Trouble, mister?"

Owen nodded cautiously.

The man said, "We heard the shots. Figured maybe one of the border gangs . . ." He glanced beyond Owen at Kate, and Matt, at Quade and at Tilton's body on the ground. He said, "I'm Jared McFee. We got a herd a few miles back. This all the crew you folks got left?"

Owen nodded.

McFee said, "You hold your herd right here. We'll catch up an' let 'em trail with ours."

Owen said, "I'm obliged."

The man nodded at him. He rode past Owen to where the others now stood grouped. He looked at the body on the ground. "Ain't that Beecher Tilton there?"

Quade said. "It is."

McFee grinned. "He won't be missed." He swung his gaze to Kate. "Your herd, ma'am?"

Kate nodded silently. Relief was so strong in her

face that Owen thought she was going to burst into tears.

"You just hold em' here till noon, ma'am. We'll pick 'em up with ours an' take 'em on to Abilene."

"Thank you. I don't know how—" She glanced at Owen and then said firmly, "We'd have made it. But thank you, anyway."

McFee nodded, turned and rejoined his men. The group rode south.

One thing yet remained that must be done. Owen said, "Matt."

Matt glanced at him. The boy still looked shocked and sick, but color was gradually returning to his face. Owen said, "Let's take a walk."

He walked away toward the open, grassy plain. Matt followed and after several minutes, caught up with him.

At last, Owen stopped reluctantly. He didn't want to stop and he didn't know how to say the things he had to say. He began. "It's been a rough drive, hasn't it?"

Matt said stoutly, "Not too rough."

Owen's throat seemed to close. He glanced quickly at Matt and then away. "Know what that was all about back there?"

"I reckon Mr. Tilton was tryin' to steal Kate's herd."

"You blame me because he's dead?"

"No, sir. You didn't kill him."

"I tried. Only, Quade beat me to it."

Matt was silent. Owen glanced at him again and stubbornly met the boy's eyes. He said, "Beecher Tilton was blackmailing me. He was there when your father was killed."

Matt's eyes pinched down and his face lost some of its increasing color. Owen said bluntly, "I killed your father, Matt. I was sent to bring him back. I called out to him and he whirled. I thought he was going for his gun."

Matt still remained silent, avoiding Owen's eyes, and Owen added almost defiantly, "I was the deputy in Tilton's story, Matt."

He knew he had done a bad job in the way he had told the story to Matt. He wished he could have done better. He had bungled it and maybe if he'd said the words differently . . .

Desperately he said, "Matt, I thought he was resisting arrest. I still think he intended to." And he waited then, for there was nothing more he could add. He had told the simple truth, awkwardly perhaps, but as best he could.

The wait stretched out interminably, but at last Matt said, "Let's go back, Owen."

He stared at the boy. He could see no hate in Matt's young eyes. He could see no change. He said, "Matt . . . you don't hate me because I killed your pa?"

"You said you done the only thing you could. You wouldn't lie to me." Matt swallowed. "Reckon it was like back there." There was a long moment between them, a long moment while Owen blinked his burning eyes. Then Matt asked again. "Now can we go back?"

Owen turned his face away. He swallowed and swallowed again. He clenched his hands into fists as he fought for self-control.

The years with Matt had borne their fruit. He needn't have worried at all. He hadn't needed five years more.

He said, "Uh huh. We can go back now, Matt."

He walked through the knee-high grass with Matt and suddenly the sky was bluer, the sun brighter than he had ever noticed them being before. He walked with Matt toward the slight, strong, gentle girl in baggy outsize clothes, waiting for them to come back to her.

Her eyes clung closely to Owen's face as they drew near, seeking an answer, and when she found it, she turned her glance to Matt. "He's a big man, Matt, with a big heart. Do you think there is room in it for both of us?"

A moment of silence, of waiting. Then Matt was nodding his head, and grinning, and a flood of sudden tears came to Kate's anxious eyes. Owen folded them both tightly in his arms, where they both belonged.